INFRACTION

USA TODAY BESTSELLING AUTHOR

K.I. LYNN

INFRACTION

I WOKE TO THROBBING PAIN THROUGHOUT MY BODY, A POUNDING headache, and the sound of my name. It was faint, but growing in intensity as it moved toward me.

My eyes opened, and I looked around, seeing the door of what I recognized as a hospital room.

"Lila! Lila!" Nathan's voice cried out. It was a frantic, panicked tone I had never heard before.

"Lila!"

"Mr. Thorne! You need to return to your room!" was screeched at him by who I assumed was a nurse.

"Lila!"

"Don't pull that out," another voice scolded.

"Lila!" he wailed, and it sounded like he was on the verge of tears.

It was clear he was ignoring the nurses as his search for me continued; they were threatening to call security.

"Lila!" he called out again, desperation flooding his tone. He was louder, only one room away.

My chest tightened, and my heart began beating at a furious pace.

Seconds later, his hands appeared on the doorway, bracing himself while his eyes searched for me.

I gasped when I took in his appearance; he was wearing nothing but a hospital gown. One tube hung from his wrist, hanging down on the ground.

His expression was what had me in shock and my heart wrenching. Tears streamed down his pink cheeks; his eyes were wide and frantic, a look of despair overpowering all other emotions.

As soon as his eyes met mine, his body relaxed, and his face morphed into one of relief and joy.

"Lila!" he cried out once more, stumbling toward me.

He reached out and grasped onto the sides of my face, his forehead leaning onto my bandaged one.

"Oh, thank God. Thank God, you're alive."

Warm tears landed on my cheeks as he continued mumbling. I stared at him in stunned silence. This was not the Nathan I knew. The mask was gone, and for the first time I was seeing the true Nathan without any inhibitions. He was raw and lay bare before me.

He was stunning. More beautiful than usual in his agony.

I didn't move, I didn't speak, I lay there stunned. He was crying.

Nathan was crying.

One of his tears dropped, sliding down to my lips. My tongue peeked out to lick it away, and my taste buds danced, registering the salty evidence, proving I wasn't imagining it.

"Nathan, what's going on?" My voice was thick, my throat dry, and I began to wonder how long I'd been out.

He pulled back from me to look into my eyes. "You don't remember?"

I shook my head and immediately stopped when I found how much it hurt. My vision spun, and my eyes were having trouble tracking.

"You were in a very bad accident…" he trailed off, and his eyes moved from mine, looking over my whole body.

I could tell I was hurt—the throbbing and shooting pain when I tried to move was proof enough without the excruciating breaths. His expression told me I was as bad off as I felt. His fingers ran over my gauze covered arm. I realized my whole arm was wrapped when he pressed his fingers to mine. He moved back up to my head, inspecting the bandage and gauze that was wound around it. With light strokes he ran the back of his fingers against my cheek, and even that hurt. I was certain I didn't want to see a mirror at that moment.

He stayed clear of my leg, which was good as I might have punched him if he touched it because it hurt so much already.

"I'm so sorry. This wouldn't have happened if I…"

His being there, his pain, made me angry. His apology even more so. "If you *what*? Hadn't left me? Broken me? Left me a shell of the paper thin person I already was before you? If that's even possible."

"All of those. I can't tell you how sorry I am."

My jaw clenched, another thing I found painful, as annoyance took over. "You didn't do this physical damage to me. What you did was far worse."

"Please, Lila, please!" he begged in a whisper.

My chest felt like he was stabbing me with a knife, and in an angry fit I lashed out. "Please, what?"

"Please, I'll tell you everything, anything you want to know if you… Can we start over? I need you so much."

My tone was harsh. "Why? Why did you leave me if you were going to beg for me back?"

"I'm so sorry I did this to you, to *us*. I was trying to protect you, and myself."

"Protect you from what exactly? What did you need protection from?"

"From losing you the same way I lost…my wife," he admitted, his eyes screwed tight.

I swallowed hard, absorbing his words. There was a twinge in my chest that had nothing to do with my injuries and everything to do with him. My anger subsided for a brief moment, but bounced back.

"And what were you protecting me from?"

"From the Marconi family." His eyes were boring into mine, beseeching me to understand.

My eyes widened. The Marconi family was well-known for their criminal connections. Their reach was mostly the northeast part of the country.

I was hesitant with my next question as I wondered what he'd been involved with in the past. It left me wishing I'd read those articles about Nathan instead of closing them down. "Why would you need to protect me from the Marconis?"

He sniffed and another tear slid down his cheek. "Because if they found out about you, they would kill you like they did her."

I stared at him, slack-jawed. He'd mentioned his condo wasn't in his name. It was evident to me now it was part of his hiding. "Why did they want to hurt her?"

"They were trying to kill me."

"Oh." My lips pressed into a thin, taut line. My head was pounding, and as much as I was happy he was opening up, I just wanted him to go.

"I can't let that happen to you."

"So you let me go? Were you ever going to ask me what *I* wanted? Were you ever going to tell me and let *me* decide for myself to risk my life to stay with you or cut all ties? Do you feel anything for me?" I needed some answers right then, though I wondered if they would be enough.

"I feel *so much* for you. I tried to stop it. I knew it could happen with you—I sensed it from the beginning. The pull I feel to you is so strong. I tried to will myself *not* to develop these feelings for you, but you just won't fucking be denied!"

"I don't understand what the fuck you're saying," I grumbled.

"I'm saying Darren was right. I tried so hard to deny it, to deny *you*, but he saw it. He said I was being selfish by leaving you, that I did it because I didn't want to be hurt again, that I was a coward for it. He was right. He saw it from the moment he arrived at the hospital when you were unresponsive."

My brow scrunched. "Dr. Morgenson? How do you know him, and what did he see?" My patience was running thin, and Nathan's head shook, making it worse. "Just fucking say whatever it is you're trying to say!"

My chest protested, screaming at me, and I laid my head back down. The pain was almost unbearable.

He looked at me, his face torn as he studied my features. His mouth opened and then closed again, the words stuck.

"He knew that I'm in love with you."

My eyes widened, my mouth dropping in shock as my brain attempted to process what he had said.

"I love you, Lila," he declared. "I'm so scared about what that means for you."

My heart skipped a beat as words I had longed to hear

slipped past his lips. The problem was they were tainted by the darkness he had carved in my heart.

I laughed; it was a harsh one, my bitterness soaking through, and he flinched in response. "You love me? Then why did you leave me?"

"I'm sorry, I..."

"You love me? You're sorry? Do you somehow think that makes everything better?" I asked, my voice growing in volume despite the protest in my lungs.

"No."

"Then what, Nathan? What the fuck do you want?" I asked, tears welling in my eyes. I needed to know. He needed to tell me. No more hiding.

"I..." he began, and then shook his head, his eyes pleading with me for some sort of unknown understanding.

"Out." My right arm lifted, despite the pain, and pointed toward the door. The chance was given for him to give me something, anything, but he didn't take it.

"Wait, Lila, please," he begged.

"I said get the fuck out!" The action of yelling caused my eyes to grow wide as an agonizing fire ripped its way through me, my injuries protesting my movements.

My breaths became shallow, each harder than the last. The beeping on the machines increased.

Nathan stepped toward me, and I growled at him in warning. "No! Out!" My hand grabbed hold of the ice water on the stand next to me, and I threw it at him. The lid popped off when it crashed into his chest. The cold water spilled all over him, and he wore an expression of utter shock while the sound of the plastic, hitting the hard floor, filled the room.

I screamed out, the pain from jostling my body so intense

a white light clouded my vision. In the background, Nathan was calling to me along with other voices, coaxing me to calm down, but all I could pay attention to was my own gasping breaths and shooting pains coursing through my body.

I was crying out in pain between the pants. Every sound I emitted caused the stabbing in my chest to flare, which would cause me to scream yet again. It was a vicious cycle.

It took a while, but with the help of some drugs, I regained a normal breathing pattern.

"Ms. Palmer... Delilah, I'm Dr. Thomas. Do you recall how you were injured?" he asked, and I shook my head. His hand reached out and stopped the motion. "It's okay, not too much. Now that you're awake, I'm hoping we can better assess your injuries. As of right now, we know you have a broken leg. You also have multiple lacerations that we've stitched up. We're going to evaluate you and go from there, all right?"

I nodded in response, and nurses began taking new vitals while fingers poked and prodded me. I may or may not have hit one of the nurses when my leg was bumped, but thankfully they understood.

For what felt like the next millennium, I was examined and moved about, left with nothing but my thoughts to keep me company. The nurses tried to draw me into conversation, but I wasn't paying attention. What had me was him: Nathan. Everywhere in the hospital I went, I could still feel him. My eyes searched for him as they wheeled me down corridors. I never did see him, but I knew he was near. After everything, there was still that rope that bound us together, pulling me to him.

Sixteen hours, seventeen x-rays, and one CT scan later, the tally was in: bruised ribs, broken tibia and fibula which needed surgery to be realigned with a metal rod to hold the bones together, sprained left wrist, a concussion, and a linear skull fracture. To top it all off, I had multiple lacerations to my arms, legs, and head, and bruises with various scratches that covered my body. I was also informed I would not be leaving the hospital until after the surgery to fix my leg. My surgery was scheduled for Tuesday, and if I was lucky, I would be released on Wednesday.

It was going to be a very long week.

They gave me lots of medicine for the pain, and I soon found myself drowsy. After a small fight I gave up trying to stay awake and fell into a deep sleep.

Soothing strokes of my hair woke me sometime later, and my eyes fluttered open to find Caroline staring at me with wet eyes.

"Caroline?"

"You gave us quite a scare, sweetie," she said with a sniff. Her fingers continued to run through my hair past the bandage that circled my head. "How are you feeling?"

I attempted to move, but my body protested by shooting pain throughout, including my lungs when I breathed. "Like I've been hit by a truck."

"Full size work van."

"Huh?"

She smiled at my confusion. "You were hit by a full size work van."

"Oh. Well…that hurt, probably more than a truck."

Caroline tried to suppress a laugh, but it came out anyway. "I bet it did. Do you remember?"

I shook my head, an action I found to be bad when my head began to spin. "How long have I been here? I know the doctor came in, and I had all those tests after Nathan..." I trailed off, my brow scrunching as I remembered how he was dressed. Not in his normal tailored suit, but in the same drab hospital gown I was wearing. "Why is Nathan in the hospital?"

She pursed her lips. I knew she wasn't happy with him and all that had gone on with our breakup, but there was something in the look upon her face. She was...torn.

"It's almost seven in the evening on Friday, you've been asleep for most of the day, and you've been here for almost two days. Nathan, well, he ran, literally ran to you after you called him... Lila, were you aware he was in a car accident?" she asked, avoiding answering my question.

"No, but I figured that was probably what caused his scars."

She stared at me for a moment as she processed that bit. "And his wife?" she asked with reluctance.

"I just found out he had been married and that she died."

She contemplated for a moment as if she was wondering exactly how much to tell me. "I made it to the accident scene because I was getting off the elevator when Nathan was rushing on, and he said to Jack that you were in an accident. I followed after him, running as well, which you know how hard that is in heels. Anyway, when I got there he was calling out your name; the police were trying to move him back behind the line. You were unconscious on the stretcher and you..."

"Caroline?"

Tears slid down her cheeks. "I thought you were dead. There was so much blood. Nathan saw you and lost it. He had a massive panic attack, which I wouldn't have known the signs of if it wasn't for you. It was...terrible to see, much worse than when I watched you. They had to sedate him before, I don't know, he had a heart attack or something."

"Why?" I asked, confused. Why did he care?

"Why what?"

"Why was he having a panic attack?"

She stared at me with her eyes wide before she leaned in. "Lila…because he thought he'd lost you; he thought you were dead."

"He didn't have me to lose." My breathing picked up as the emotional pain tightened my chest. "He threw me away."

A pained expression crossed her face. "As much as I hate him for hurting you, I think…I think he's in love with you."

"He said that."

"He did?" she asked, surprised.

"Yes, but I don't believe it."

"Why not?"

"Why would he throw me away if he loved me? I've been thrown away and thrown around and none of those people loved me," I said, my eyes trained on the ceiling.

Her fingers were shaking as they glided across my arm. "People sometimes do it when they love someone."

"So, you're telling me that all people throw you away, whether they love you or not? Why do I want to live in a place like that?" My chest was screaming at me. I tried to lie back and calm down in hopes it would help, but the movement caused my leg to jostle, and I almost passed out from the combined pain that cut through me.

It was time for a new dosage of pain meds.

"Please don't talk like that," she begged.

"Why? You're telling me it doesn't matter; I'm going to be thrown away anyway! I should have killed myself when I was younger. That van should have done me in!" I cried out, tears streaming from my eyes. I struggled for breath, the pain unbearable.

"Lila…" Caroline's voice faded away, a tear falling down her cheek.

"Don't you ever fucking say that again!" Nathan's voice growled from the door.

I gasped and turned my head to find Nathan, eyes blazing with fury, standing in the doorway with a few people behind him. The action was too fast. I was hit with dizziness, my head falling back onto the pillow.

In a flash he was standing over me, his features concerned. There was so much force behind his expression I wasn't sure if I could handle it.

"Please, don't ever say that again… Don't leave me, Lila."

His fingers brushed against my cheeks, and I had to forcibly stop myself from leaning into his touch. It hurt, but in a different way. My heart fractured again at the look on his face I caused. My gaze moved to anywhere but his eyes. That was when I noticed he was back in his suit, minus the tie.

"You left me," I said.

His fingers dropped, his hand returning to his side. "Let me explain. Please? I need you."

"Sorry, I don't think I'm fit to help you out at the moment," I sneered, turning to look up at him.

I was going to go into a rant, to dig into him more, but the expression he wore stopped me. The mask was once again gone, and I was astonished by the emotions emitting from the man in front of me. The pain he held was visible, etched into his perfect features.

"I'll make it up to you. I promise," he said in a low voice.

I didn't respond. I couldn't. There was no response. He'd never promised me anything before. The word had never slipped past his lips.

A throat cleared behind him, and I craned my head around to see his father standing next to a woman with dark brown hair speckled with grey and a soft, sad smile. Another woman with the same dark hair was also with them, and Andrew made up the rear.

"It's getting late, Nathan. We need to get you home," George said.

I felt a tugging at my waist and glanced down to find Nathan's hand fisted in the thin hospital blanket and my wonderful hospital gown.

"I...please?" Nathan begged.

Sadness washed over the older man's face. "Visiting hours are over, and Lila needs to get some rest."

Nathan stared back at his father, beseeching him.

While he did that, Caroline stood from the chair and leaned forward, placing a kiss on my forehead. "I'll be back tomorrow, okay?" Her hands smoothed the hair from my face. "I love you."

I squeezed her hand. "Bye. Love you, too."

She walked toward the door, glaring at Nathan as she went.

"I'll be back around lunch to check on you," she said upon parting through the crowd and exiting.

"Lila," the older woman began, "I'm glad you're okay."

I stared at her for a moment before remembering my manners. Even if I didn't know who she was, I still needed to be polite. Teresa would be disappointed otherwise. "Thank you."

She gave a tight smile before exiting as well, George right behind her.

"I'll be back in the morning," Nathan said. I roamed my eyes back up to him, one of the few things that didn't hurt to move. He leaned down and also placed a kiss on my forehead. My heart hammered in my chest at his closeness. I wanted to tilt my head up and capture his lips in mine. But I couldn't. I wouldn't.

He walked out the door and my chest seared, but for a different reason than the bruised ribs. Moisture filled my eyes before flooding down my cheeks.

From my periphery, Andrew's tall, lanky form walked over to me.

"What do I do?"

He pursed his lips. "You should hear him out, let him explain. That way you can make a decision based on all the facts."

"You know, then." A statement, not a question.

"Yes. I made a call to an old friend in the D.A.'s office. You need to hear what he has to say. I don't like what he did to you, but I have a better understanding of why he felt he needed to do it and…" he trailed off and sighed. "I can't hate him for that."

He took my right hand, my good hand, in his. His long fingers dwarfed mine as they always had. "We'll all be in to see you at some point in the morning. We all love you and want you to get better." He paused, his expression torn. "That includes him, you know."

I nodded, and he squeezed my fingers before turning and walking to the door. "Hey Drew?"

"Hmm?"

"Thank you."

"You're welcome. Now get some rest. I know you haven't been unconscious enough today," he said with a wink and a wave goodbye as he disappeared.

It was quiet then, the beeping of the machines and the aching pain the meds didn't dull down my only company.

I stared at the ceiling and contemplated Nathan's request to hear him out and wondered if I could. I didn't have anything else left to lose; he'd taken what little there was of me. So what harm would it be? Maybe then I could understand and begin getting over him. I still didn't believe he wanted me. He felt guilty, was all.

Doubt crept into my mind as I replayed his frantic pleas in my head and the three words he had spoken most vehemently.

"I love you."

The words swirled around in my head, and I didn't even notice the nurse when she entered to take my vitals. I did, however, notice the new meds she slipped into the IV, because my eyelids grew heavy, and I drifted back into unconsciousness.

T WAS A FUN-FILLED MORNING IN THE DRIEST SENSE.

I awoke in pain—something I knew was going to be my constant companion for the months to come. As soon as the nurses knew I was awake, they pumped me full of more pain meds. The drugs helped, but made me a little on the loopy side.

Not what I needed to be when my first guests of the day arrived: police officers. They'd come to take my statement in regards to the accident, and unfortunately I was unable to recall anything. The last thing I remembered was running out to my car in the rain and then waking to Nathan calling my name in the hospital halls.

They asked me where I was headed, did I see the van, was it still raining, what color was the light? Standard questions, but I was getting more and more annoyed with their attempts to get some answers out of me other than the only one I had: *I don't remember anything.* They weren't going to jog my memory.

Got in the car, woke in the hospital. End of story.

It surprised me when the officers questioned me about the call I had made to Nathan before the paramedics arrived. I had no recollection of it at all, but I remembered Caroline mentioning the previous night I had done so.

After a few minutes, they grew frustrated with my non answers and left, stating they would be in touch. I knew they would, but I still didn't have any answers on how I ended up here besides what I'd been told.

An hour after the police left there was a light rapping at my door, and I looked up to find the older woman with the gray-streaked brown hair standing in the doorway.

"Good morning, Lila. Might I join you?"

I blinked up at her. "Who are you?"

"I'm sorry we haven't been properly introduced. I'm Sarah Thorne, Nathan's mother," she said.

I was a little hesitant, but she had a sweet, infectious smile. My head tilted as I looked at her, taking her in before speaking. "It's nice to meet you. I take it you already know who I am?"

She nodded. "And I must say, after George told me about you, I dreamed of meeting you. However, I never envisioned our first meetings to be with you in a hospital bed."

"You dreamed about meeting me?" I asked in wonder.

"Of course! We've all been waiting for Nathan to return, and when I heard he was in a relationship, I couldn't contain myself." Her smile faded. "Though I never thought our first meeting would be while you were in a self-induced coma because of my son."

I scrunched my brow and thought back to that time. There was a faint memory of an unknown voice. My eyes widened. "Oh! That was you?"

She blinked at me. "You remember me?"

"I remember a voice that spoke to me in a different emotion than the other unknowns."

"Well, when I heard you had no one and Nathan was there all of the time—"

I interrupted her. "Wait. What about Nathan?"

"You didn't know?" she asked, genuine surprise in her expression.

"Know what?"

"He spent every free moment they would allow outside your hospital door."

I was in shock from her revelation. Not only that, I was pissed. I had suspected he was there, and she had just confirmed it all.

"I know you're upset with him, it's written all over your face, but I want you to know and realize he didn't abandon you," she said, her tone urging and pleading with me. "Let him explain, let him tell his story. I hope when you hear all he has to say you'll try to forgive him."

"I can't promise you anything."

"I'm not asking you to. I'm imploring you to hear him out, before you write him off for good. He cares so much for you."

"Okay." I hoped she was right, but I had my doubts. Nathan walked away, not me. Was I supposed to act like he hadn't kicked me to the curb like garbage?

I felt confused. I wanted to believe her so much—every fiber of my being begged for it—but my heart was still bleeding out over his rejection. Letting him talk to me might be tantamount to ripping the bandages back off my gushing, wounded heart. How would I survive?

I was already a step away from being completely obliterated by him the first time he ended things with me. Wasn't being in the hospital proof enough for them? Yet, his mother sat in front of me, begging me to hear him out.

I closed my eyes and tried to calm my fraying soul.

Just listen to her, Lila. She seems like a nice woman, and she's a mother. She wouldn't do anything to hurt you…

That thought died as an image of my father, Steven, popped into my head. He was supposed to be the one to protect me and love me, but he'd hurt me the most.

No, she's not him. Stop thinking that way!

I took in a slow, even, measured breath, opened my eyes, and tried to silence my mind, focusing on what else she might want to say to me. She took the time to visit me; the least I could do was listen to her.

She steered the conversation away from Nathan and me and into a more neutral territory by asking about me. I was grateful for that.

We'd been talking for a little while when I heard my name being called by a familiar voice. I turned as Teresa ran through the door.

She was frantic, her words reverting to Spanish. "Ay dios mio!" I only caught about every third or fourth word, but the overall gist of it was understood. "Mi niña!"

"Teresa, it's okay. I'm okay, calm down," I said, trying to soothe her.

Tears ran down her cheeks. "Oh, Lila, when Andrew finally got hold of me this morning and told me what happened…my sweet girl." Her hands caressed my face and hair. "You look a mess!"

I grimaced. "I figured as much."

"Andrew says you were hit by a reckless driver."

"That's what I hear."

"You don't remember?" she asked. I shook my head in response. "Well, I'm here now, so if you need anything, okay?"

"What about your newbie?"

"He'll be fine. He's in school today, and he has a cell phone. Kids in this day and age. Though, I would have felt a lot more secure knowing you had one. I always dreaded that he would come after you…" she trailed off, her gaze lifted from me, and she blinked. "Oh, hello."

Sarah smiled back at her before leaning forward and presenting her hand. "Sarah Thorne."

Teresa smiled back and took the offered hand. "Teresa Desanto. I'm sorry, I didn't mean to interrupt."

"Oh, no, no. I'm just here to keep Lila company and her mind off of her injuries as best I can."

"How sweet of you," Teresa said, a smile brightening her face. "I'm so happy to hear Lila has met such nice people."

Teresa moved back and pulled over the other chair in the room to sit next to Sarah. There was some small talk, and more about my injuries revealed to Teresa, along with tales from Spain. Teresa let me know Armando sent his love, and he was coming home in the next week.

Most of the visit I spent listening. I was too tired to concentrate on conversing, and didn't have anything of importance to add. I was pretty sure I drifted off once or twice. It made me happy Sarah and Teresa were getting along so well; I could hear in their tone their genuine interest in one another, and it set me at ease.

My head lolled to the side, and I looked out the doorway, watching the people walking back and forth. I stared in wonderment when Nathan entered through the door behind a nurse. I was shocked he'd come back. He was dressed in jeans and an old gray Harvard Law tee that clung to his body just right. I tried not to lick my lips at the sight, but it was no use.

It was lucky I was able to pull it off that my lips were dry, and nothing more. My audience remained oblivious to my ogling him. Why did he have to look so good? Butterflies swirled in my stomach as I remembered the loving words he'd spoken to me, while my chest tightened over the memory of the pain he'd inflicted not long before that.

I once said he was a contradiction, and I was beginning to see I was becoming one myself, at least where he was concerned.

"Nathan!" Sarah said, smiling up at her son.

"Hi, Mom," he greeted, bending down to kiss her cheek.

He straightened up and our eyes met. His façade was back on, but I watched it fall away as soon as he looked at me. Walking forward, he smiled; I was confused as to why he did that. Upon reaching me, he leaned down and pressed his lips to the top of my head, his hand cupping the side of my face.

"Good morning, beautiful."

I quirked my good brow at him. I scoffed, "Yeah right."

"Lila," he said in a warning tone.

"Look, this isn't one of my 'down on Lila' moments. I was hit by a fucking van. My eye is almost swollen shut. The left side of my face feels as big as a beach ball and hurts like hell. So that tells me I look like someone used half my face as a punching bag. Don't think I'm very beautiful at the moment." I knew I was pretty bad off; I didn't need a mirror to tell me that.

He let out a frustrated sigh. "You are always beautiful, even when a van uses you as a punching bag."

I stared up at him for a moment before looking down at the tube in my hand. Why did he have to be sweet right now? I needed to be mad at him, but he kept saying and doing things that were chipping away at my resolve.

"Oh!" My head popped up as I remembered we weren't alone. "Teresa, this is Nathan. We...um...work together. Nathan, this is Teresa."

I knew no more introduction was needed; he knew who she was. He had an excellent memory, and his eyes lit up with recognition.

"Teresa, it's wonderful to meet you." His hand reached out to grasp hers.

She stared up at him, looking mesmerized. Not that I blamed her; he had that effect on me quite often.

"It's nice to meet you, as well," she said in automatic response, still confused as to who he was. I hadn't even had any time to mention him yet.

Nathan leaned against the bed near my head as the chairs were occupied by his mother and Teresa. His fingers, every once in a while, would run through my hair or touch my arm.

Teresa looked from me to Nathan and back. "So, Nathan, what brings you here today?"

The room went eerily quiet, and I found myself very interested in the dots on the ceiling tiles.

"I mean, that isn't the greeting you give someone you work with," she added. "And it isn't customary the mother of someone you work with comes to keep you company while you're cooped up in a hospital."

Nathan let out a small, nervous laugh under her gaze. His hand rubbed at the back of his neck.

My stomach rumbled, and Sarah snapped up to her feet. "Lila's hungry!" We all turned to look at her, but she didn't seem to care that she sounded a bit psychotic in her outburst. "Come, Nathan, let's go get her some good cuisine, not the yucky hospital food. You remember how bad that was. Let's allow the two of them to get caught up without any interference from us."

"But I just got here," he protested.

"Now, Nathan." It wasn't a request; it was a demand from his mother. He couldn't disobey that.

"I'll be back," he said, leaning down to kiss my forehead again before following Sarah out the door. I stared after them for a moment, then turned back to Teresa.

"All right, what in the world is going on between you two?"

I sighed as best I could, cringing a little before charging into our sordid tale. I began with him coming to work, the office romp, the growing feelings, and topped it off with the demise of "us" and ended with his declaration two days prior.

"Wow." She sat back in awe once I was finished. "That's quite a history you two have." I nodded in agreement. "What now?"

"I…I don't know. I just don't know." Even I could hear the sadness in my voice. I didn't have a response. My heart still hurt so much, and I couldn't trust him. I was angry with his declaration. Why couldn't he have told me two weeks prior? Why did he now have a sudden epiphany and need to be with me?

"We've got Italian!" Nathan smiled as he walked back into the room carrying two bags, Sarah trailing behind with another bag, and Caroline bringing up the rear. "Oh, and we found Caroline."

"Hi!" Her tone was bright as she walked over to give me a small hug. "Hi, sweetie. How are you feeling?"

I groaned.

She let out a small chuckle. "I don't think that's a word. Can you use it in a sentence?"

"That would take more brain power than I have at the moment."

Sarah, Teresa, and Nathan were chatting as they unloaded the bags and divided up the contents. I stared at them…well, him…and the way he interacted with them. There was an ease about him I wasn't used to. Almost as if some cloud had been lifted from him, still guarded but somehow free.

He held two containers in his hands as he walked toward me, setting them both down on the table beside me and going back to get another object along with some utensils.

"I got you some lasagna. I figured it would be easier for you to eat," he said, popping the lid off the containers.

The smell hit me and my stomach growled in want. He smirked, holding a fork up to my mouth. I reached for the fork and he pulled back.

"Give it to me. I can feed myself. Just set the container on my lap." I waited, but he didn't move, the fork still an inch from my mouth.

"First off," he began, "the container is too hot to sit on your lap. Second, you can't use your left arm, and you think I can't see your right arm is stiff today? You pulled some muscles, so even if I moved the table in front of you, it would be difficult. And how are you going to cut it? Third, I'm just as fucking stubborn as you are, so open your damn mouth." I set my jaw despite the pain, unwilling to do as he requested, and glared up at him. His hard eyes softened and he sighed. "Please, let me help you do this. I just want to help you."

I looked over to Teresa; she was urging me with her gaze and mouthing words to me. With great reluctance my mouth crept open, and he slid the fork between my lips.

I moaned when the flavor hit my taste buds, my eyes

rolling back. Two days with little food, hospital food at that, made the bite heaven and my stomach happy. My greedy mouth devoured the whole lasagna, my stomach more than full once done. Somehow, I still had room for the mini cannoli he placed at my lips; the sweetness was the perfect end to the meal.

We were all talking after eating when the nurse came in with another round of meds. Soon I found my eyelids heavy, fighting against the light.

The next time I awoke, Nathan was beside me, his fingers making light trails up and down my good arm. He was humming something, but I couldn't make out the tune.

An involuntary twitch in my hand caused his head to rise, and he smiled when he saw I was awake. Picking my hand up, he brought it to his lips and placed a light kiss on the scrapes.

"Today any better?" he asked, his hand reaching up to brush a strand of hair from my eyes. His fingers lingered a while on my skin, and I leaned into his touch.

"We'll see. It's a little bit easier to breathe than it was four days ago, so I suppose that's an improvement."

"You'll be out of here in no time," he said. "You won't have to worry about a thing; we're going to take care of everything." I looked at him in shock. He hadn't implied what I thought he had. "We decided it's best for you if you stay with me, where you will have friends and me to take care of you."

My expression morphed, and I resisted the urge to yell out, knowing that would cause me great pain. "No."

His brow scrunched in confusion. "*No*? No, what?"

"Look, I'm not going to fucking sit here and have everyone

make decisions for me. I'm a grown woman, and I can take care of myself. I have a mind of my own; I don't need you."

He shook his head. "You're not in any physical position to help yourself right now. You need round-the-clock care."

"Well, I think I can manage to set that up myself. They have services for that."

His spine straightened and his lip quirked up in a snarl. "Fuck services. You have friends and people who consider you family—who *want* to help take care of you. You can't do it on your own."

My teeth mashed together as I glared at him. "Like hell I can't."

I was about to continue, but we were interrupted by the sudden entrance of an unknown person.

"Oh, good, you're up!" I recognized her as the woman who was with his parents a few days ago. "Lila, I brought you a change of clothes and some toiletries from your condo."

I stared at the woman in front of me, trying to recall if I knew her. Did I have amnesia? She was addressing me as if she already knew me.

"I think I'm hallucinating. Do you see her, too?"

Nathan sighed. "Yes, she's really there."

"Okay," I said and turned back to the strange woman. "Who are you, and how did you get into my condo?"

"Oh! Sorry! Erin Morgenson. I'm so happy to finally meet you." Her hand grabbed my good one for a small shake. "Also, don't worry, but I did some laundry so you have clean sheets, and I made sure all pathways were clear."

"Erin!" Nathan said with a hiss.

She stared back at him. "What? It's not like you were in any shape to do it."

"She's going to stay with me."

I lay there and watched the odd conversation unfold before me, lost in what was centered around me.

"She can*not* stay there! Not with the 'redecorating' you've done." Her fingers made air quotations for the word.

"Redecorating?" I asked, and they both turned to look at me.

Nathan's jaw tightened and he held a pained expression, while Erin's was a little frightening, in a maniacal sort of way.

"Erin," Nathan growled in warning, but she just shrugged him off.

"He lost it and tore down all the dry wall with his bare hands the night he left you."

His fist slammed down on the bed next to me. "Damn it. Always sticking your fingers in things."

Erin rolled her eyes. "She has a right to know just how crazy you are about her. And, fuck, it's been years; let me have a moment of finger sticking."

"What you just described sounds psychotic," Nathan said with a huff.

"I'm no expert there. Should I get Darren?" Erin asked in a sweet, condescending tone.

My brain was still processing what all I had heard in the last hour and that bit pushed me over the edge. "How the fuck did you get into my damn condo?"

They stopped their childish argument, then Erin turned to me and squeezed my hand. "Your friend Caroline; we were getting it ready for you."

My brain hurt. I was so confused. "Why the hell were you there? Who are you?"

"This is my cousin. Sorry, she lacks manners."

"Oh!" It clicked into place.

All I could think about was how everyone was making decisions for me and treating me like a child. I looked between Nathan and Erin, and with each turn of my head my expression soured and my anger grew. These two, one I didn't know and the other who threw me away, were going to make decisions on my behalf? They knew what was best for me?

Oh, hell no.

I'd spent the first half of my life with people making decisions for me, from how I acted to how I would feel about myself.

Who did they think they were? Did my opinion matter at all? Was I going to have any say in what my life was like and who my time was spent with over the next who knew how many weeks?

The answer was no.

I lost it.

"Out!" Nathan's head snapped to me, his expression full of shock and fear. "I said get out!"

"Lila, please." He reached out to me, but I pulled away as best I could. "Not this again! You need my help whether you want to admit it or not."

My heart broke further from the pain that flooded his beautiful face from my reaction. Hadn't he destroyed me enough? He said he loved me, but with all that had happened in the last two weeks, did he really expected me to just forget? I wasn't so desperate I could flip that switch. He hurt me, deeper than anyone before. From what had transpired over the last half an hour, I knew he had hurt himself, as well.

"I'll leave these here for you," Erin said with a sad smile, placing the bag on the empty chair next to the bed.

My chest burned, and I struggled to breathe.

"Lila," he began, but I stopped him.

"I said get out!" I couldn't stand to have him there at that moment.

I watched the two of them walk out, Erin dragging Nathan backward by the arm.

The nurse walked in a moment later, and she cursed under her breath about them upsetting me. I was gasping for air, and seconds later she added something into my IV.

I welcomed the sweet relief from the pain. The relief I felt from not thinking was what I welcomed most. I'd heard too much about Nathan and the pain he was in, which pointed to his declaration being true. That was bad; that could spark hope, and the last thing I needed him to give me was hope.

Especially if it had anything to do with him and my heart. I was done being hurt.

STARED AT THE SPECKLED CEILING TILES, COUNTING EACH IRREGULAR dot in my boredom. I'd been at it for hours.

There were 516 on the tile directly above my head.

I felt like Edmond Dantes from *The Count of Monte Cristo* in that moment, in his cell on Château d'If.

If there was a hell, I was certain I was in it. Half crazy, all broken, pain radiating through all of my body and soul.

Nathan's words didn't help. I'd accepted that he didn't want me, that he was through with me. Part of me wanted to run into his arms, but another part reminded me of the pain from his heartbreaking note.

Round and round I went with myself, neither side winning. The only thing I could do was count the holes, since I had no answers. I was halfway through the tile to my right, the fourth in my dive into crazy town, when a light tapping on the door drew my attention. I glanced to the door with my eyes, not wanting to move my head, and found the heat had been turned up on my hellish fire.

"Can I come in?" Erin asked in a small voice.

"Why?"

She took a step into the room, and I scowled at her. She halted her movements, her hands fidgeting with her purse.

"Lila, I wanted to apologize for the other day. My behavior with Nate was unacceptable, I, well… I was happy."

"Happy?" There was a definite edge to my voice.

She held up her hand. "Let me explain, please." She walked forward and sat on the chair at my bedside. "I was happy, not because of what happened to you, because that was horrible, and not for what he did, because I kicked him in his bad shin for that."

I fought a smile as I envisioned his pain, but it also made me sad he was hurt. Internally I hung my head; it was pathetic how much I was in love with him.

"I was happy because, for the first time in four years, I could see light in his eyes and a sweet smile on his face. Nate is like a brother to me; we're practically twins," she said with a smile.

"You don't look anything alike."

She let out a laugh. "Well, he's only two weeks older than I am, and we were inseparable as kids. My parents were often out of the country, so I spent half my time at Aunt Sarah and Uncle George's. We went to school together from preschool all the way up until college. If we hadn't had different last names, most kids in school thought we were twins. He then went off to college and got married, and I gained a wonderful sister."

I found myself smiling along with her, the image she was creating in my mind so different from the one I knew.

Her face darkened and filled with sadness. "And then that night came. I was on duty in the ER. I saw them w-wheel him in." Tears began to fill her eyes and spill down her cheeks. "I only recognized him by a scar on his palm I gave him when we were kids. There was so much blood. His eyes were open, just slits, but they were empty. The side of his chest and abdomen were torn open, his leg and arm mangled and pointing in all the wrong directions."

My chest constricted as she spoke, making my already difficult and painful breathing worse. I could see everything; I knew all of the scars that were proof of the damage she described.

"I was the one who had to contact everyone, and when they got there, I collapsed, unable to hold myself up anymore. The wait was excruciating. Surgery after surgery to put him back together, and on top of that, they kept him in a coma for weeks. When he came out of it, Nate was gone," she said, choking back a sob. "I lost my best friend and my brother, and no matter how much I fought to bring him back, he slipped further and further away. When they brought him in the other day, I threw up, thinking it was the call I had been waiting for all these years. I was shocked when Uncle George told me it was because the woman he was in love with was in a bad accident, and he'd suffered a severe panic attack. When he woke up, he was in such a fury to find you, and in that moment, light broke through the clouds that covered me since that night."

She took my hand in hers. "I know he hurt you, and you don't know why, but you will. I just ask that you think about forgiving him and give him a chance to show you the kind of man he is. I know you're one of Darren's patients; he's my brother-in-law. I don't know anything about you; I only know he works with trauma patients. I've heard from your friends how your relationship was healing you, and I know it was healing Nate. To get back to my original topic—sorry, I ramble when nervous—we're all happy you're here. Well, not here in the hospital, but that you met Nate. You give us hope, something we'd pretty much given up on. Thank you."

I stared at her for a long moment. "Thank you?"

"For giving us back hope. Am I forgiven for my horrible behavior earlier? Do you understand now? I was overexcited, and my timing was just pretty bad."

I surveyed her and found her to be mostly harmless before I held out my good hand. "Delilah Palmer."

Her whole face lit up. "It's such a pleasure to meet you, Lila."

"You, as well."

"So, when you get your cast on, can I be the first to write on it?" she asked, excitement sparkling in her eyes.

"How old are you?" My lips curled up into a smile.

"Oh, come on!"

"No."

Her bottom lip jutted out in a pout. "Nate wouldn't let me either. Though it wasn't fun then."

"It isn't fun now!" I shook my head. "What in the world would you write anyway?"

"Hmmm," she paused for thought, her finger tapping on her lips. "Oh! How about this: Nathan and Lila sitting in a tree, K.I.S.S.I.N.G. First comes love, then comes marriage, then comes Lila with a baby carriage."

I stared at her in disbelief, and then shook my head and smiled. "You're crazy."

"Shh!" She leaned forward, her hand to the side of her mouth as she looked from side to side before continuing. "Don't tell my husband. My kids know, but they've been threatened with Brussels sprouts at every meal if they say anything. My youngest likes them, so I had to threaten him with lima beans."

"How many kids do you have?"

She beamed at me and pulled out her wallet. "We have two boys. Brennan is nine, and Alec is five." She flipped it open and showed me a picture of two little brown-haired boys.

Erin and I continued to talk for another hour. She told me all about her kids and her husband, Trent. They were contemplating having a third child; Erin really wanted to have a girl. Then conversation moved to her growing up with Nathan.

"Oh, we used to get into so much mischief. He was the leader of course."

I let out a little chuckle. I could totally see that.

"He was a wild child, but I blame Aunt Sarah for some of our antics."

"Why is that?"

Erin laughed and shook her head. "She pumped us full of sugar. I swear, that stuff is like speed for kids. I don't even let mine have it very often. This one time, we were about six, and he found some pixie sticks hidden in the pantry and we stuffed them all down. Half an hour later, he was running around the neighborhood screaming 'I'm too sexy for my shirt, so sexy it hurts' butt naked."

Nathan walked in then, glaring at Erin. "Shut up. It didn't happen."

Erin winked at me. "I've got the photos his mom took."

"I'll have Trent find them, and then I'll burn them."

"That's fine, but I also know where the video is your mom filmed as Uncle George started chasing you, trying to catch you. Full-Monty. And I know how to use YouTube now."

Nathan shut up after that, but it was obvious he wasn't happy.

I laughed, feeling lighter than I had in weeks. They were

very amusing together. A spark of jealousy flared in me. If life had been different…

We spent the next few hours talking, sharing stories. Erin and Nathan had a much better and fun-filled childhood in comparison to my own.

I relaxed as the conversation morphed, and I got to see a different side of Nathan.

A nurse came in after a while to shoo them out; visiting hours were over. She also came to give me the next round of drugs, and back under I went.

My eyes fluttered open for the billionth time in the last who knew how many days. I had been in and out of sleep and everything was running together. I wouldn't know if it was day or night if it wasn't for the southerly facing room I occupied.

It was Monday…no, Tuesday. *Right?*

I sighed in frustration. They needed some sort of countdown on the calendar where I could read it from where I was situated. All I knew was that it was six, or so said the clock on the wall above the door.

"Good morning," Nathan's voice called, pulling my attention down to my bedside. It was rough from sleep, and it reminded me of mornings when things were different. Times when I felt safe, our bodies intertwined as we shut away the world and it was only him and me.

There he was, in a different suit than I'd last seen him. His hands were wrapped around my good one, tracing light circles on my skin.

He'd gone back to work that week on a reduced hours capacity. Caroline and Andrew filled me in on the meeting Jack had on Friday describing how Owen, the intern Kelly accosted with a coat rack while leaving our office one day, was filling in for me.

They also mentioned how Jack made up an interesting story as to why Nathan was out and working less over the next few weeks.

It fell very much in line with real life, including telling people he'd been in an accident where he almost died, and hearing I was in a bad accident sparked the memory and induced a panic attack.

Once again, I wondered how much Jack knew.

Jack had come to visit once, when Nathan wasn't there, to check up on me. He let me know that while things weren't quite up to my standards, they were chugging along and I needed to concentrate on getting better and not worry about the office. I also was informed I would not be returning to work for at least two weeks, and even when I did it would be part-time for a few more. I had plenty of sick time built up over the last few years, but he said he already had the FMLA paperwork in the works if needed.

"Morning?" I asked in a scratchy voice. Ah, yes, the sun coming from the left side of the window.

Nathan smirked. "Morning."

He handed me my water, and I took multiple large, greedy gulps. "Thank you," I said, handing him back the half empty cup.

"You're welcome."

"I probably stink." The thought popped directly from my head to my mouth.

He chuckled. "Why do you say that?"

"I've been here for over a week and haven't had a shower. I'm peeing through a tube. My hair has been washed with dry shampoo, and I've had a couple of sponge baths, but I just feel gross and can't wait to get home," I said while trying to be sly and sniff my hair, which he caught. I wanted a shower in the worst way.

"About that," he began, his hand reaching up to rub his neck. "We're working on getting everything ready for your release. We've mapped out a loose schedule so you're never without anyone."

"What?" I questioned, blinking up at him. Schedule? "We're? Contraction for 'we are.' As in more than one. We as in a group of people?"

"That way someone will always be around if you need anything," he replied.

I stared at him in disbelief. I was being babysat? "I don't need anyone's help. I can take care of myself."

"Really?" His voice was laced with sarcasm and anger. His jaw tensed. "You can't even walk! How are you going to get to the bathroom? How are you going to get your meds on time? How are you going to eat?"

"I can do it alone. I've taken care of myself my whole life, and I can do it now. I don't need your help!" My lungs protested, but it wasn't as bad as it had been. At least some part of me was getting a little bit better.

"Like fucking hell you don't! The doctor says you won't be able to walk on the crutches for about three weeks, which means you're confined to a wheel chair to get around. How the hell are you going to get yourself in and out of the chair? You'll end up ripping out your stitches, and you'll be in pain from the exertion. Trust me on that."

"I can do it on my own."

It was stupid, I knew that. He was right, but I hated he'd decided everything without consulting me. I was still trying to sort out my feelings, and he was pushing himself into my life.

"Why the hell are you being so damn stubborn about this?" he asked in exasperation. Tears welled in my eyes, and his hand cupped my face to wipe them away. "Please, Lila. Let us take care of you. Let *me* take care of you. Pick another battle, but stop fighting me on this one."

"Why? Why do you care?"

"You know why," he replied, his forehead resting on mine. He took a deep breath and sat up, grabbed my hand, and placed it over his chest, over his heart. "I'm yours. All that I am, if you want it. I'm not much, but I know I can be so much more with you."

I swallowed hard. I'd never been taken care of with the exception of the time I spent with Teresa and Armando. I wasn't used to it. It felt…wrong on some level. Maybe that was because the few times my dad ever did anything like that was when we were in public, and I paid for it somehow when we got home. So, what would the price be here?

Logically, I knew there was none. Nathan and his family were doing things for me because they wanted me to get better. They all had a genuine care for my well-being, and not one born out of obligation.

Nathan's gaze was locked on something outside the room, his expression blank. My eyes followed his to the opened door of the room across the way. The window shades were open, exposing another wing of the hospital.

"Nathan?" He still had my hand in his grip, but he was lost, his mind somewhere else.

"That wing is new. Before, you could see out to the interstate. There was a gap between the buildings, and when the leaves were down you could see a glint of the art museum in the distance." His vision was still locked on the room, out the window. With a tight grip, and clenched jaw, his gaze moved back to me. "I spent six months in that room."

"In that exact room?" My voice went up in pitch and my eyes widened.

He nodded. "After that, I was moved into my parents' house where I spent almost a year. I hated having to depend on them, to depend on anyone. I got angry and lashed out at them on many occasions. I was lucky I had people who were willing and wanted to take care of me, to help me get better. You have that, too, Lila." He brought my hand up to his lips and kissed my knuckles. "You're not alone in this, and it's only for a couple of weeks until you're able to get around on your own."

"I...I need some time to think about it," I said, staring up into his beautiful blue eyes. They were mesmerizing as he spoke, and if I wasn't careful, he could have me agreeing to a lot more.

He smiled and sat back down, still holding my hand in his. It was an innocent enough gesture, and I would be lying if I said it didn't bring me comfort.

I would also be lying if I said I didn't want it and much, much more.

An hour later, Nathan left to get some food; I wasn't alone for long though, because Teresa showed up to spend time with me. I could tell she wanted to talk about something, but I wasn't sure if I could handle it right then. So much had been going on over the previous days, and I had so many drugs in my system I didn't even remember half of the conversations I had.

"He's in love with you," she said, not even bothering to ease into it. "I've been watching him for the past few days, and that statement is true whether you want to believe it or not."

"How do you know?" I wanted, I needed, someone to tell me the truth. The real truth I either couldn't, or wouldn't, see.

She contemplated before speaking. "It's the little things. He's always around."

"He feels guilty."

"He's considerate of your state: emotional and physical," she pointed out.

"He doesn't want me to get worked up."

"The soft, loving looks and touches," she countered with more force.

I blinked back a few tears. "I don't know if I can do it. I don't know if I can put myself out there, give myself to him again. How do I trust him with my heart?"

"Time. He's offered himself to you on a silver platter as penance."

Tears slipped down my cheek. "I don't want it as penance!"

"Oh, Lila," she said with a sigh, her fingers running over my hair. "He wants you. He wants to love you and take care of you. That's why he's doing all of this. For you. He wants you to know him, hear him out. Do that, and then think about it, don't just react like you have been; *think*. Then make a decision on what you want to do."

I sighed before nodding. "Okay. I'll listen."

"Good," she said with a nod. "Now that we have that settled, I wanted to go over the schedule with you."

"I told him no!" I groaned in frustration.

"And, damn it, I say yes." My eyes popped at her curse. "Delilah, you are not alone anymore. There are people who *want* to take care of you. Not because they have to, but because they love you."

I knew of all people Teresa cared for me. I trusted her, and her opinion. And to be truthful, it felt good to be taken care of, something I'd never had before. I didn't know how to handle it all, though, and reacted poorly. I felt like my life was spiraling out of control. I had control over nothing, not even going to the bathroom, and that was a very difficult thing for me to relinquish.

Control was what I had been granted when I contacted Joan to be removed from my family. I ended up a very stubborn person because I was afraid. I felt if I gave up one ounce of control, I was losing, and being in the hospital, I'd lost a lot. That was probably why I liked to give up control in the bedroom—a release from my own made chains.

"Okay," I relented. I needed the help, and I trusted Teresa.

She would be there. What I was afraid of was spending the evenings with Nathan. I didn't know if I could take being that close to him without breaking down or mauling him. Not that I had the energy for mauling.

She smiled and kissed my forehead.

"It's okay to be scared, mi niña, but I see good things, wonderful things, once the clouds have dissipated. Love is a beautiful thing."

I nodded, tears once again streaming down my face. My chest was tight, trying to hold on as I let go.

N AND OUT. IN AND OUT.

I felt like my hospital room was a revolving door. Strange that it took a car accident for me to feel wanted for once in my life. Then again, half of them were Nathan's family, people I'd just met.

The people who came did so because they wanted to see me. They were worried about how I was, if I was bored, and some were worried about my future with Nathan.

Nathan's whole family was very kind and set on keeping me entertained, keeping my mind off the pain when I was awake. The meds kept me pretty sedated, but almost every time I woke, someone was there.

Sarah, Erin, Teresa, and I could be found playing cards from time to time, or some game someone brought in. Movies came and went, and I was now caught up on many of the recent blockbusters. Well, those I didn't end up falling asleep watching, which, thanks to all the drugs, was quite often.

Nathan was always there in some capacity, with the exception of work and sleep. Many times he was running errands, usually for non-hospital food for me and whatever guests I had. I still needed time, but there was always touching. It was as if he needed verification I was alive: small caresses and kisses, looks of longing. His declaration and actions left me…confused.

I looked over to the wall, counting down the minutes until he returned, knowing the minute he showed up, I'd be counting the minutes until he left.

It was a sick game my mind played on me.

My heart fluttered when his body filled the space in the doorway, carrying a bag from one of my favorite restaurants.

He smiled as he set it on the table in front of me, leaning down to kiss my forehead before a look of guilt crossed his face.

"What's going on?" I asked, my eyes following him as he took a step back and tried to hide his cocky grin.

"Nothing." He grabbed the nearest chair and dragged it over. The legs made an awful scraping sound against the floor. He sat down on the edge, grinning at me. "Anything exciting happen while I was gone?"

"Nope." I kept staring at him. He'd crack eventually. It was clear he was hiding something, and I could wait him out.

"Shame."

"Shame you're acting like a lunatic. Did you find some happy pills in the hallway on the way in? You better tell me…"

"Well, I'm sure you're bored out of your mind when you're alone. Not to mention, how many times can you work on the puzzles in the paper, or play solitaire? I know your brain is fuzzy from the drugs and it's hard to concentrate." He was spot on there, but he, of all people, should know what it felt like.

I blinked and swallowed. "Okay, so after you took the happy pills, did you tell the doctor with the ice pick you didn't want a lobotomy? Why did you let him steal the one proper functioning part of your—"

His arm reached around to his back pocket, the movement causing curiosity to cut me off.

My eyes flew open when he pulled out a DVD from behind him.

"Did you bring me porn?" My voice broke.

"Not exactly…" He smirked and held the movie or whatever it was between his two flattened palms.

"Then what? *Homemade* porn?" That thought excited me.

He rolled his eyes and chuckled. "Come on, do you think they'd let me visit again if I brought you something like that? Besides, I know you can look that stuff up on your phone."

"Hey!" I pursed my lips and gave a mock scowl.

"It's something I had to call around to find," he said.

"Goddammit, Thorne, you're killing me here. What the hell is it?" I gripped the bars on the bed with my good hand and shook the frame a little for dramatic effect.

It hurt a little, but it was worth it to watch him spring to action.

"Honeybear! Don't do that. Are you okay?" He inspected me, checked my IV and glanced over my arms, touching them as he went. It gave me chills at the same time my stomach flipped at his term of endearment. "You didn't hurt yourself, did you?"

I gave him a pitiful expression, then when he was distracted, snagged the DVD from his grip and stuck my tongue out at him.

His jaw dropped, then he grinned and chuckled. "Brat."

"Asshole. That never seems to change—lobotomy and happy pills or not." I inspected the case to find out what it was. My whole being stopped when I saw the front.

The 1943 edition of *Jane Eyre*.

"You know you like it," he said, looming over me.

"I…I don't know what to say."

"Say thank you. That's what I was told to say after my lobotomy." He tapped his forehead.

"Thank you. But how did you know?"

It was my favorite of the classics I'd been forced to read in high school, and the only one I liked. I read it over and over and as I devoured the words, I felt like I was reading about myself in some ways. I could relate to Jane—she became my role model—and I hoped one day for my own Mr. Rochester.

In my heart, I knew I'd found him in Nathan even if my heart hurt. I dared to hope, even with as angry as I was.

"I have my ways." He leaned over and kissed my temple.

Normally, I would have glared at him for doing that, but I was speechless at his gift.

"Teresa?" He confirmed my suspicion with a nod, pressing his lips together. "That woman…" I shook my head, still smiling. I was living with her when I first rented it from the library. She sat next to me when I watched it for the first time, and didn't mind when I watched it again and again.

"It's nothing to be ashamed of. We all have our little unmentionable fetishes." He laughed.

I was pretty sure I knew all of his.

"Well, fuck, if that's what they teach you after lobotomies, maybe I need to get one, too." I hugged the DVD to my chest. "Let's keep this crazy to ourselves."

"I already told the nurses you'd want to be left alone tonight."

I grinned. I sure would.

I tucked the case under the covers, the smile unable to leave my face. There was nothing wrong with romantic fantasies, and it had been a long time since I let myself indulge in such things.

The perv loved every minute of my reaction, my face reddening with each passing second. Damn him and his goofy lobotomy grin. There was a resurgence of some feeling in my body, and I knew it had nothing to do with the drugs in my system.

I stared out at the crashing blue waves, my hands sinking into the warm sand. The sun was bright overhead, and in the background I heard laughing.

Not really a laugh, but a giggle, high-pitched and full of glee. I scanned the beach and saw a familiar brown-haired man.

Nathan.

He was off a little ways to my left, chasing a small girl. Her hair was the same light brown as his, reflecting brightly under the strong light of the sun. I moved to stand, to go to them, but my movement was restricted. I felt weighted down, too heavy to properly move.

Looking down, I found my stomach, bulging out from between my hips, round and full. Out of nowhere there was a giggling sound, pulling my attention away from the mountain that my stomach had transformed into. To my right, there was a little boy, clapping as he watched Nathan play with the little girl. The child's hair was white-blond, and when he turned to me, a warmth spread through me. Those eyes. The same deep blue color as Nathan's were boring into me. I smiled reflexively at him.

"Daddy and Anna play. I play too!" He squealed in excitement, his words slurred by toddler speech.

They heard him and headed toward us. Nathan was beaming while he watched the little girl run in our direction.

She bounded up to me. "Mommy! Mommy! Look at the shell I found!"

I took the large conch shell in my hand. "It's beautiful, sweetie," I said, admiring the colors of the recently abandoned shell. It hadn't been bleached by the sun and the salt yet. I turned it around in my hands, stopping when a glint of light caught my eye. Looking at my left hand, I found a large diamond ring surrounded by two simple white gold bands.

"Anna, play!" The little boy cried out.

The little girl, Anna, took the small boy's hand. "Come on, Jackson! Let's go!"

His little Buddha belly protruded out as he stood, dancing about and unable to contain his delight at playing with his sister. They ran down the beach toward where the waves crawled up the sand.

"Not too far, Anna!" Nathan called out while plopping down next to me in the sand. He leaned forward and captured my lips. "Hello, beautiful."

"Hi," I replied, breathless.

"Mmm, you look good enough to eat. Mind if I have a nibble? I'm starving."

At that, he lowered his head and began licking and nipping my neck. He was making funny growling noises as his head moved back and forth.

I started giggling at his actions. "Nate, the children," I hissed under my breath.

"Are fine." His actions slowed, and then his teeth sank farther into my flesh. My eyes widened, and the familiar heat that only Nathan could produce blazed through me. A moan slipped past my lips. "When we get home," he whispered in my ear, "I'm going to do bad things to you."

I licked my lips, and my breathing increased as my cheeks flamed. He pulled away, his face lighting up with a sly smirk.

I pouted. "That wasn't nice."

His head tilted back, his chest heaving, as a laugh I'd never heard from him came out. He wore a mischievous smile and winked at me before turning his attention to the two little ones who were laughing and running away from an incoming wave.

I felt a kick in my stomach and my hand flew to the spot. Nathan noticed the motion and turned to me, placing his hand on my skin. "My little girl wants to play with her siblings, huh?" He leaned down and kissed my stomach. "You're not quite done yet, little one. Soon."

I reached up and began playing with his hair. It was so silky in my fingers. I sighed in contentment, looking at what my life had become— what Nathan and I had evolved into.

It was beautiful. We were a family, a real one. My heart was soaring at the thought.

Beep.

Beep? I wondered, my hands still playing with his locks.

The strange beeping became incessant, steady. It pulled me away from the beautiful vision in front of me. I held onto Nathan's hair, refusing to let go. It was everything my heart desired.

Beep.

A bright light began to envelope everything, our children fading away. I began to panic, hearing the beeping increase as I called out for them to come back. It was so bright, enveloping everything. Taking away what I'd always wished for.

And then there was nothing but pain for a few seconds.

My eyes began to open, fighting against the glue that seemed to be keeping them shut. The morning light seeped through the windows. My hand twitched, and I felt something between my fingers. I looked down to find Nathan's familiar hair beneath my palm. His head was lying on his arm, his other hand draped on my stomach. He was asleep.

I'd been dreaming.

I studied him. There were dark circles under his eyes, and his face was gaunt. He seemed thinner, too. I hadn't noticed how terrible he looked because I refused to really take a good look at him. I didn't want to.

The dream resurfaced, and in my mind I remembered how good, how healthy, he looked. I also remembered the family we had. I had dreamed of him, dreamed of us, and what we could be.

My walls were cracking. I wanted it. I wanted it so badly. I wanted *him*.

My fingers combed through his hair, and I wondered if I'd been doing that in my sleep? Had I known he was there and reached out to him?

It wouldn't surprise me. I never could deny the draw I had to him. The more I thought about letting him in, the more my chest constricted, my breathing more labored.

It would be up to him. If he wanted me as much as he claimed, he would have to show me.

Everything.

Nothing less would allow me to open back up to him. No more hiding. He would have to let it all out before I even considered.

He stirred and my fingers stilled. His eyes opened, and I stared down at him. They closed again, and his head pushed up into my hand as he let out a sigh of contentment.

"Hi," he croaked. I didn't respond. I was muted as his blue

eyes gazed up at me in reverence. "How are you feeling?" His hand rose from my stomach and moved a strand of hair from my face.

"You really want an answer to that?" Just because he brought me food and movies, did not mean everything was wonderful.

"That bad, huh?"

I shrugged as best I could. "Broken heart, broken body, and broken soul. Not sure I can get more broken than that."

He cringed against my words. "I'm going to work on fixing all those things."

"You have a plan for that?"

"It's formulating. Slowly, but it's coming."

I quirked my brow at him. "Are you sure about that?"

"It's a twelve-step program."

My lips twitched. "Really? What's step number one?"

"Admitting I'm in love with you…to you and myself."

I stared at him, unable to respond, but my heart was beating at a furious pace and, thanks to the heart monitor, Nathan was aware of it, as well. "Step two?"

He let out a hard breath and sat up, my hand falling from his hair, and he took it in his. "Gather the strength to tell you about, well, everything."

"How long will that step take, do you think?"

"I'm hoping by the time you're released I'll have a plan in place."

"That doesn't give you much time."

He shook his head, lips pressed together. "No."

"That's only two steps."

"Well, I'm thinking groveling will come into play some-where," he said as he stared off into the distance, lost in thought. "I'm going to push my fears down, if step two works, so we can move onto step three."

"I wish I knew what your fears *are*," I whispered.

He lifted my hand to his mouth and kissed my knuckles. "Soon. As soon as we get you home." He glanced up at the clock on the far wall and looked back to me. It was almost eight. "I have to get to the office." He scooted back from the bed. It was then I noticed he was dressed in a different suit from yesterday.

My brow scrunched, and even that hurt. "How long have you been here?"

"A few hours," he admitted. "You have surgery prep soon, and then Caroline will be in around lunch. That should be around the time you wake up. After that, my mom and Erin are going to keep you company until I get out of work."

I winced, not wanting to think about being under for surgery. Especially knowing I would be facing it alone. No one would be right outside the surgery doors praying, pacing, or waiting. I swallowed the fear down like a cold, hard lump. My eyes slid closed for a moment, to brace myself, buoy my courage back, and keep it surfaced long enough to get through the ordeal of more trauma on my poor mangled body.

I opened my eyes and tried to focus on the strong, striking features of his handsome face. What if this was the last time I saw it? What if I died on the operating table? No, I couldn't. I wouldn't. And it didn't help to let these morbid thoughts be entertained for even a second. *I will see you again!*

"Oh, okay," I responded. It was all I could say. I didn't want to break down.

He leaned down and kissed my forehead, then with hesitance, moved down to my lips. He thought better of it before we connected and slid to my cheek instead.

"I love you," he whispered in my ear.

He turned and walked out the door, glancing back at me before disappearing.

Tears welled in my eyes as everything we talked about looped through my mind. I wanted to say "I love you, too," but that wouldn't do either of us any good. I wanted the dream.

Soon after, a nurse entered my room and began talking to me about my upcoming surgery. I could hear what she was saying, but I didn't comprehend most of it.

I was too scared to think straight—I'd never had surgery before.

Nathan, our children... I focused on the dream I had. I needed to go to a happy place and the dream was my new fantasyland. Surgery was too overwhelming to think about. In order to keep from crying, I said my phantom family's names over and over again.

Anna.

Jackson.

Baby girl in my tummy, whom I loved as much as the ones running circles around my beach ball belly.

And Nathan... *Always Nathan.*

Would they wait for me, and be my future someday?

It was all too terrifying to think of, but the warmth, the love I felt on that beach in my dream was so real. More real than these harsh hospital walls I was staring at.

The nurse said something about calming down and taking some deep breaths. That was when I realized I was borderline hyperventilating.

It all became a blur after that. Before I knew it, I was in the operating room and the anesthesiologist was telling me to count to ten.

I only made it to seven.

AWOKE GROGGY, MY HEAD SWIMMING, EYES UNFOCUSED.

"Nathan…" I mumbled. My eyes refused to stay open, my head lolling back and forth. "Nate!"

My breathing was hard. Where was he? I needed him.

"Shhh, I'm here, baby," he called, his voice rough. I felt his hand on my cheek and then sighed, leaning into the warmth.

"Take me home," I said weakly.

"What?"

"I want to go home."

"Oh, Honeybear, soon."

"Please." Tears began to stream down my face. "I want to go home. Take me home."

My eyes opened a tiny bit, and his brow was scrunched up, sadness etched in his features. He looked up at something, and a voice chimed in letting me know we were not alone.

"It's the drugs," Dr. Morgenson's familiar voice said.

Dr. Morgenson had been in and out during my stay. We had mini sessions together. To most, it would look like a normal conversation, but what was actually going on was Dr.

Morgenson playing his Jedi mind tricks on me. Some worked, others didn't, and I was always left feeling emotionally drained. He was taking advantage of my drugged state, I thought, planting seeds and pulling weeds.

At least that was how I looked at it.

"Okay," I said, answering the unasked question.

"Okay?" Nathan asked, confused.

"Okay. I'm okaying the schedule."

Nathan's face lit up and a smile began to spread before quickly fading. "You don't know what you're saying right now. We'll talk about it when it wears off."

My anger spiked, and I unleashed it upon Nathan. "I fucking said I want you to take care of me, and that's your response? After everything? I'm agreeing, so you better fucking accept it before I take it back!"

"Nathan, it's not the right moment to start arguing with her. She's not lying. She may be loopy and out of it, but she means it. Let her be," Dr. Morgenson said.

My head spun a little. I knew what I was saying, but it was coming out all wrong. Nothing made sense in my head except what I was *trying* to say.

His eyes were wide, and I could tell he didn't know what to do with me. Hell, at that moment *I* didn't know what to do with me.

I sniffled; my emotions were everywhere. "Don't you want me? You said you wanted me."

"That's not it, baby. I just want to make sure it's what *you* want."

I pulled him to me, as close as possible. I had an overwhelming *need* to be close to him. I felt disconnected from myself in some ways. Tears streamed from my eyes, and his arms wrapped around my torso, his head buried into my neck.

"I love you," I said, my breath hitching. "I love you so much. Please, please take me home. I don't want to be here anymore."

He pulled back to look at me. It hit me what had slipped past all the walls in my mind and heart, and through my lips. The deepest feelings I kept from him. Words I was afraid to tell him, the feelings that tore me to shreds and broke me to pieces when he left.

He buried his face back into my neck. "I love *you*, and I'll wait. I know you're saying things due to all the meds in your system right now. I'll wait until the day you want to say them on your own terms."

We stayed like that for a few minutes, and as the time passed, my mind began to clear. I froze with realization. Nathan's arms stayed wrapped around me, unwilling to let me go.

He pulled back and moved the chair closer, touching me the entire time. "I want to take care of you; I want you to come home with me. We'll go at whatever pace you want, though."

His finger made soothing circles on my skin, and I couldn't take my eyes off him. The world fell away, and it was only Nathan and me, at least until Dr. Morgenson cleared his throat.

"Now that I have your attention, both of you, there are some things we need to go over," he began. The doctor was in. "I've drawn out a schedule for the both of you. I think it would be a good idea, considering all that has happened between the two of you, that you have a joint session, once a week, on top of your own."

"Why?" I asked.

"Getting you both back into therapy is a necessity right now. You two need to communicate everything if you ever want to try to be together again. Otherwise I'm afraid of what could happen down the line."

"Darren, she's not even out of the hospital, so maybe we should wait on the therapy."

Anger flashed across Dr. Morgenson's face for a brief moment. "No, Nathan. We've all coddled you for far too long and it's done you no good. I'm not making that mistake again. You have to bring it all into the open so you can move on and heal. You will never heal like this; you can't even talk about her or the accident four years later! It's the only way you two can ever be together."

"I...ugh!" Nathan let out a strangled cry.

"Please, stop." I couldn't stand to see him in pain.

"He wasn't the only one to suffer from that mass of metal and glass," Darren said, shaking his head. "You weren't the only one who lost that night. They lost you as well, Nathan. Your whole family has mourned your loss for the last four years. Your mother has been fighting severe depression, but you don't see that because you never see her anymore. Erin has nightmares of seeing your bloody, broken body with your heart barely beating. You were in a coma and didn't see the devastation it caused your family, and I'm including her side when I say family. When you woke, they had to relive it all to tell you what had happened. Horrific memories haunted them every day as they helped you during your rehabilitation. That night tore your family apart, and only you can put them back together. I believe Lila is the key to that healing."

Nathan's eyes were squeezed tight. "Darren, please, no, I can't deal with this right now."

"Have you told her how it affected you to see her on the stretcher, her car a crumpled heap?" Darren turned and asked Nathan, his voice holding an edge I had never heard before.

Nathan shook his head. "Please," he begged in a low voice.

"This is what I'm talking about. If you want her back, then you need to start talking to her. Tell her about your panic attack, tell her about your dead wife, tell her what she does to you." The pain and frustration was visible in his eyes. It wasn't Dr. Morgenson I was looking at. It was Darren; Nathan's close friend.

"Darren, I…"

"Show her the box. It's the best way for you to tell her. Let her in; let her *know* you and the truth. It'll help you both." Darren's face was filled with genuine care and concern as he stared at Nathan. "If, after all she learns, she still wants to be with you, you'll have to not only accept and embrace it, but you'll have to let go of your fears. See how this works? There has to be some vulnerability for her to trust you again. Otherwise you will hold your relationship back. Let go. It's time to live."

With that, Darren walked up to Nathan and squeezed his shoulder before leaving us alone. Silence prevailed as he mulled over what to say.

"I promise I'm going to tell you. Just give me a little time," he said softly.

I nodded in response, having nothing left to say.

It was in the late afternoon three days later that I was released. Nathan helped me into the car, and as we drove away I waved goodbye to the gathering of people who had come to see me off.

The ride home was silent; I was lost in my thoughts. We were about halfway home when my hand twitched, and I realized at some point I had grabbed for Nathan's. He didn't say anything, didn't move, but his thumb was drawing lazy circles on mine.

When we arrived, he left me to get the wheel chair out of the trunk before helping me onto my new mode of transportation for at least the next week. My other injuries prevented the use of crutches for a while.

The familiar static charge was in the air when we rode on the elevator, and I was very happy I wasn't standing next to him. Instead, I fidgeted with the hospital tag I was still wearing around my wrist.

"I want to tell you," he said as he wheeled me down the hall to my condo.

"Okay." My eyes stayed trained straight ahead.

"Now."

I nodded and swallowed hard.

He found something to prop the door open as he helped me in. We moved to my bedroom.

True to her word, Erin had indeed cleaned up. The blankets were gone from the couch in the living room and were returned to the spare bedroom. My own bed was made with new sheets, the floor clear of any debris.

Nathan picked me up, placed me on the bed, and began positioning the pillows around me. He helped prop me up against the headboard, making sure my leg was elevated and then he headed out to the kitchen, returning with a glass of water that he placed on the night stand next to me.

"I'll be right back," he said, and I nodded.

In his absence, my eyes drifted around the room. Nothing

had changed, but so much had. I waited in silence, not moving. Moving was painful.

It didn't take long for him to return, and when he did, he was carrying a wooden chest about half the size of the carry-on sized suitcase he rolled in behind him.

He climbed on the bed next to me—the box was in his hand and his eyes were locked on the clasp. I heard him swallow hard, and the butterflies in my stomach multiplied. That was what Darren had been talking about.

"I h-haven't opened this in over three years."

"What's in it?" I asked in a whisper.

His hand moved over the lid, his voice a whisper. "Ghosts."

With trembling hands he flicked the clasps and tilted it back, opening the contents to the world.

My jaw dropped when my eyes landed on the picture that lay on top. It was the first thing I noticed because I recognized the photo in question. It resided in Jack Holloway's office. Well, most of it did. Jack had hidden the third person in the picture. It wasn't only his daughter and him; it included Nathan.

"That's Grace Holloway, Jack's daughter."

"Yes," he agreed and swallowed hard once more, "but, her gravestone reads Grace Thorne."

My eyes snapped to his. "Oh, my God."

"There are a few at the office who know, those who have been around long enough. They know, but have been asked not to say anything about it."

I couldn't speak. Shock shut my mind down.

Things Jack said came back to my mind. I was still new when his daughter had died in an accident. He had grieved heavily for her, and I remembered being confused by some of his behavior due to my own experiences with my dad.

I remembered talking to Dr. Morgenson about my boss's behavior.

My stomach dropped. Darren had to explain the grieving process to me like I was a child. A process he and his extended family were going through over the same loss as my boss.

"We were married after we finished our undergrad. When I went to Harvard, she came with me and got a job, working while I attended classes. It was a bit of a strain, as I know you are aware law school is, but we made it through. After Harvard, we moved to Indianapolis and found a house and talked about children. Grace always wanted a big family," he said, his shoulders slumping while he fingered through the box. "Four miscarriages. She made it to the end of the first trimester only once, and it was ripped away."

Thoughts about having children had never crossed my mind before the dream, so to even think about wanting them and then losing them was lost on me.

"When she finally made it to the second trimester with her fifth pregnancy, my trial of Via Marconi ended. In all my bravado, I failed to recognize the danger I put my family in. I managed a conviction of a Marconi family member, something that had never happened before. Not only that, it was the daughter of the head member of the family. All the time away from my wife and the nights without sleep, working eighty plus hour weeks while I gathered as much information on them as I could, paid off in the end."

I remembered that trial. Young, hotshot prosecutor had done the impossible, they said. "Rising star," they called him.

"Vincent Marconi wasn't too pleased, and I gloated in his face," he said through clenched teeth. "Fucking stupid."

I couldn't think of anything to say, so I slipped my fingers in his, giving him any comfort I could.

"It was about two weeks after my birthday that we went to Grace's parents' house for a combination Father's Day and my belated birthday celebration. Her whole family and my parents were there. That was when she gave me this: the first glimpse of my son." With shaking hands he handed me a framed photo.

The frame was wracked; the corners loose and bent. Evidence of the glass could still be seen in the powdery sand in the edges and the scratches on the picture in my hand. The ultrasound picture was in such bad shape it was difficult to read the printed words "I'm a boy!" I swallowed hard; he'd been so close to having a child.

"Not even that survived unscathed."

My eyes looked up at him. "It happened that day," I said, the answer coming to me, filling in the gaps. Nathan hated it when I mentioned his birthday.

He nodded in response. A sad smile formed and his arms raised, his hands making a circular form. "She had a perfectly round stomach. We'd made it to the third trimester after so long."

Grief was what overtook Nathan. I recounted the stages in my mind: denial, anger, bargaining, depression, and acceptance. Nathan was still stuck on step four—depression—along with his up and down visits with two: anger. It was obvious to me now he'd never moved on from there. Even after four long years, step five, acceptance, remained out of reach.

He sat there for a moment, and I could almost see the memories flickering behind his eyes. His jaw clenched a couple times. "It was just after dark when we decided to head home. It wasn't too long a drive, about forty-five minutes, from their house to ours. There was a two-lane road that was almost a straight shot and a nice drive. We were about halfway home when this car came up behind us fast. We weren't in any hurry, so I pulled over to let him pass. But when I pulled over, so did he."

My chest tightened. I knew what was coming. The end. I knew the outcome.

"That was when it was obvious something was wrong. I told Grace to hold on and gunned it when I saw the driver's side door start to open. We were up to seventy in no time…but so were they."

He tipped his head back, trying to keep the tears at bay. I squeezed his hand in mine, my eyes beseeching him to continue.

"My mind was racing with what to do while I tried to stay ahead of them, but soon we were passing eighty. By then we'd reached the point where the road ran parallel to the interstate. They were separated by about forty feet of grass and a wire fence. It was then the fight of our lives started. They caught up, going faster to catch up in the oncoming traffic lane. I glanced over and the window was lowering. There were two men; the one in the passenger seat was aiming a gun at us. I reacted on instinct and steered the car into theirs. The motion caused them to lose some traction and they ran off the road, but were soon gaining on us again."

He paused, his gaze on the box, his hand absently moving the objects around. "I remember telling her I loved her, but that's where it gets foggy. An eye witness, who was silenced, said that was when the struggle began. Our car and theirs battled back and forth to stay on the road. With a powerful hit, they pushed us off the road and we went through the grassy area and the wire fence into oncoming traffic on the interstate. We were clipped by a semi, thrown into the median wall, bounced out, and hit a sedan before a delivery truck mashed us into a bridge support."

My whole body was frozen in shock, my hand covering my mouth.

"All my fault," he whispered as he stared blankly into the box. "It was all my fault."

"Why?"

He blinked up at me. "Because I baited them, flaunted my success in their face, gathered enough information to begin bringing down their organization. Once I had one, the others would be easier. People would see even they couldn't get away with everything." He sighed. "In the end, they could. The eye witness's testimony, the bullets they found—all evidence disappeared under mysterious circumstances. It was labeled an accident, and I 'lost control' of the vehicle."

"Are they still…after you?"

His gaze met mine and he stared into my eyes, his hands bringing mine to his lips. "Yes."

"Why?"

"Because of what I hold. The information I have on them. When I started poring over all the evidence for the case, it became a rabbit hole and I was able to link it to more and more cases." He shook his head. "I wish I didn't have it anymore so they would leave me alone."

"Why don't you get rid of it?"

"Because it wouldn't make a difference, and because they died for it."

"Are you sure they're still after you?"

He let out a huff. "It's been a while; I think they like seeing me miserable. In a way they think it's better than being dead because I've suffered a worse fate than his daughter. But, yes, they still keep tabs."

My fingers shuffled through the items in the box: pictures of them in college, their wedding day, their home. It was all he had left of her—a wooden box filled with paper and faded memories.

I stared at one of the photos, and something Jack had said to me long ago came back.

You remind me of my daughter.

"I'm not her, you know." His brows scrunch together in confusion at my words. "Jack said I reminded him of her."

He thought about that for a moment, his head nodding a bit. "I'll admit there are a few similarities I noticed in you in the beginning, and it was one of the many things that drew me to you. But then I saw you, *really* saw you, and it was then it hit me you weren't her and the similarities were just that. No different than how you are."

"What do you mean by that?" I asked, the hackles on my neck standing up.

"I've been watching you for months. You shy away from bald men," he said, ticking off more subtleties I'd never noticed myself. "You cringe at men wearing combat boots. Why?"

"Adam always wore them, especially when he kicked me. My dad went bald at an early age." My voice was mechanical as I answered, and my chest tightened, the walls reinforcing themselves, so I redirected. "It's the same with you, though. If I cringe from them, you are drawn to me. These photos show our similarities. You can't refute it."

His lips formed a thin line. "When I first saw you at the

office, the physical similarities, your hair color and size, even some of your mannerisms were hard to distinguish. Over time I saw the pain behind your eyes, the emptiness." He paused and looked to me, his fingers ghosting over my cheek. "I saw the mask you wore."

He took a deep breath before continuing. "I resigned myself to a solitary existence. Convinced myself I would never love again. And then you came crashing into my life. You didn't fawn over me like the others, and you saw through my façade into the man hiding inside: destroyed and angry."

"You slipped around me."

"I did," he agreed. "You do that to me. I tried to ignore you for weeks. I saw it in you, the same pain and loneliness in myself. At first I thought it was because you reminded me of Grace in some ways, but then, after the first few times I was with you, I realized that, while it was something that drew me to you in the beginning, it no longer applied. I wanted you, craved *you*. I struggled every day with that knowledge. You saw the evidence. I pushed you away, along with the pull and feelings you were stirring within me. But when I took you, I gave everything I could and it was raw and primal. I craved you to the point of insanity."

I pursed my lips, the war raging inside between wanting to believe him and wanting to protect myself. "Are you sure? Are you sure that's what you're feeling? Are you certain you aren't using me as a replacement for her? If she was alive, you would still be with her, not me. You don't really feel about *me* the same way I feel about you."

He stared at me for a moment, trying to form words for feelings. "I'm struggling with the realization of my feelings for you. What it means for you and for me. I never thought I'd fall in love again. Then I met you, and no matter how hard I pushed you away or how much I tried to not feel anything, it didn't do any good. If I believed in fate, I would say I was destined to meet you; that I had to go through all this so I would understand you and see you."

I thought about it for a moment. The feeling I had was the same, like something tied us together. "It's a force, but is it love?"

"I loved Grace, very much, and I'm struggling with guilt over the fact I love another and you could mean more to me than she did. That I want you more. That this connection we have is greater. To be honest, it scares me, because I would be decimated if anything were to happen to you, especially if it was because of me. Every time I said I didn't want you, it was me trying to convince myself."

"What about your nightmares?" I asked, finally having an arena to ask a long wondered upon thought.

"My nightmares?" He paused and looked deep into my eyes. He was gauging me for something, but I couldn't tell what. "They were about losing you, seeing you dead. The day of your accident, I saw one of my nightmares come to life."

My chest constricted, and I was on the verge of crying. "Why wouldn't you tell me any of this before?"

"Because I couldn't admit it to myself, but your accident split me open and made me look—at you, at us, at the feelings I was trying to disown. The thought that I lost you…well, you saw."

"You've had a session with Dr. Morg… with Darren, haven't you?"

He nodded in response. "I refused to acknowledge how I felt about you. I thought if I didn't admit it to myself, then it wasn't true and you would be safe from them. That backfired and made you unsafe from me. Darren helped me to realize everything I kept closed off. I was angry at myself and the situation I created. You didn't deserve to see that anger." His hands fidgeted with the fabric of his shirt that lay over his heart. "I want to live again…with you. You've changed my world. I'm altered, no longer stuck in purgatory."

Tears welled in my eyes before they began to slide unbidden down my cheeks, hot and heavy. His hands moved to my face, thumbs gently wiping the small beads from my skin.

"After seeing and hearing all this, do you still want me? Do you want to try, really try?"

I thought about it; my mouth opened to say yes when something nagged at me. That voice I knew so well in my head. *You'll always be second best in his heart.* I sat back and slumped against the pillows.

"No," I replied in a whisper. I watched the hope drain from his face, his jaw clenched tight. Tears welled in his eyes, and I took his hand in mine. "I can't be a replacement. I won't be. You haven't had closure and until then, after all that has happened between us, I need to matter more than a memory. Not only that, I don't know if I can let you back in. You hurt me more than anyone else has in my life."

He nodded. "I understand. A small part of me wants you to tell me to fuck off, because I'm afraid. I've only ever loved my wife; this is all new to me. I don't want you to be hurt or killed because of me…because you're with me. At the same time I don't want to let you go, I won't. I need you, so bad. It's your decision to give it a try with me, to be in a real, healthy relationship. If I'm honest, that scares me almost as much, but I promise to work at getting better, and I won't push you away anymore."

"How do I know I can trust all that?"

"I've never made you any promises, because that would be confirmation of the feelings I wouldn't allow myself to have. So I buried them." He picked up my hand and placed it palm down on his chest over his heart. "As cheesy as it sounds, this changes now because I'm promising you—my heart is yours."

My brow scrunched together. "Not all of it."

Sadness washed over his features. He couldn't deny it.

WE LAY THERE FOR A WHILE, ME ABSORBING EVERYTHING, Nathan taking in my answer. I scratched at one of the scabs on my thigh and looked down. My legs were hairy and had bothered me all week. It shouldn't have, but what else did I have to think about after I was done counting the dots on the ceiling? It hit me that I was home now; I could bathe.

"Nathan," I began, breaking the silence. "I want a shower."

I turned to look at him, and he nodded. "Okay."

Climbing off the bed, he moved to my side and picked me up, carrying me into the adjoining bathroom. Once there, he sat me down on my good foot, careful not to bang my bad leg on anything before stripping me of my clothing.

"Hold on to my arms."

It was then I got my first good look at myself in a mirror.

Just when my bruises had finally disappeared, I had a whole new horrifying set.

My face was just as bad off as I thought. Black and blue had turned to yellow and purple and covered the left side of my face from where I'd hit the glass window. Part of my hair not far above my ear was shaved off to get the area around the laceration on my scalp cleaned and stitched. My arms also held varying shades of bruise, darker around the countless number of stitches that held my skin together. Not too much longer until those came out.

My focus moved to the other figure in the mirror. Nathan was stripping, and my eyes went wide. I was about to ask him what he was doing when I recalled the state I was in; I wasn't going to be able to shower on my own.

It was the first time I'd seen him without his clothes on in nearly a month, and I hated to think about how much I wanted him right then. It was like his body was calling to mine, and mine was desperate to answer, as always.

Perhaps I shouldn't have felt that way with all that had happened, but I still felt the pull to him. I was such a mess, my mind and heart both having two different opinions; the push and pull was exhausting.

Once we were both naked, he helped me to sit on a stool that had been brought in. I didn't ask because I noted a few new items around that, when I thought about it, were all to help me in some way.

He pulled some rubbery looking thing over from the counter and began stuffing my casted leg into it, being as careful as he could.

He looked up at me and smirked at my expression. "This will seal off your leg so no water gets into your cast. You really don't want that. Trust me."

"Oh. Okay." I sounded stiff and off to my own ears, but I wasn't sure how else to respond. I hadn't even thought about something like that, and he had it ready to go whenever I was.

He had planned everything out for my arrival home. I didn't know how to react to something I wasn't used to, but it did make my chest clench.

He moved to the shower and turned it on to warm it up. Tears prick at my eyes. I wanted to wrap my arms around him, feel his lips on mine, and forget the last month had even happened so we could go back to how it used to be.

I was lying, and I knew it. I wanted to know everything he had told me, the honesty he displayed. The man in front of me was not the man I had known a month ago.

I took in a deep breath.

"Lila?" I looked up at him; a tear escaped and slid down my cheek. His face twisted in pain as he walked over to me. "Come on, the water will feel good." He bent down and carried me into the shower.

I was grateful for the first time that my shower had a built in bench, because I was already exhausted from the previous ten minutes. He sat me down, the spray hitting me all over right away. It felt so good to have the water running over my skin. I felt cleaner already, just from the spray drenching me; it was the cleanest I'd felt all week.

Nathan grabbed the handle on the removable shower head and I placed my hand on his, directing where the spray would go. After a while I kept it over my head and let it fall down my body, my muscles relaxing; the tension rolling away with the water.

He soaped up a washcloth with my body wash, but before he connected with my skin I pulled it from his hand. He looked down at me, startled.

"It's the only independence I have at the moment," I said, explaining the need to do it myself.

He nodded in agreement. "Sorry, I got a little carried away."

I scrubbed my body as clean as I could, making several passes. All the movement left me winded and he didn't want to hand me my razor, but when I pleaded, he relented. I couldn't stand being furry any longer.

I was drained by the time I was done, the most physical activity in over a week I had participated in. Nathan hung the shower head back up after wetting my hair again and grabbed the bottle of shampoo. He applied some to my hair and sat down next to me.

His fingers tangled in my hair, working up a good lather. My eyes closed, and I moaned a little; I always loved my hair being played with. He was careful on my stitches and avoided that area of my scalp as best he could.

The movement of his hands stopped, and my eyes opened again to find him pulling the shower head back down to where we were sitting and began rinsing the suds out.

I looked up to him and found him studying my face. One of his fingers reached up and lightly traced the outline of my fading bruises.

His eyes met mine, and in the depths I could see everything. His pain was on display full force after our conversation. Had my bruises brought his memories and fears to the forefront? Tears welled in his eyes before one spilled down his cheek. He leaned forward and rested his forehead on mine.

My hand reached up to comfort him; his stubble was coarse beneath my fingers. He clenched his jaw then dipped farther down.

For the first time in over three weeks, I felt his lips against mine. It was soft, yet hungry and full of a familiar fire.

Too much. The feeling was too much, and I had to pull away.

He nodded in understanding, but it didn't keep the pain from showing.

A few minutes and a dose of conditioner later, we were done. I hadn't felt so good or clean in over a week.

Nathan exited the shower and came back with a towel wrapped around his waist and one in his hand. He helped me stand and began drying me off a bit before carrying me back out to the stool in front of the mirror where he removed the blue rubber boot from around my cast.

Sure enough, the cast remained dry.

He finished drying me off and toweling my hair before taking me back into the bedroom and laying me down on the bed. He located a fresh set of sleep shorts and tank top and helped me into them.

His eyes lingered a bit on my skin, but that was all. The normal aggressive, sexual beast was kept away, and all that remained before me was a broken man.

He arranged the pillows to where I was comfortable again, then left to get me a fresh glass of water and my next dose of meds for which I was happy. I was getting accustomed to being in pain, but the medicine helped take the strong edge off and left a lingering dull ache.

I noticed every move he made, every conscious decision to make me more comfortable to sleep.

Such a simple act, but I could *feel* it.

A tear rolled down my cheek, and then the bed shifted with his weight. He was next to me.

"Are you okay? Do you need more medicine?" he asked, his fingers wiping away the salty droplet.

"I'm okay, just…rough day."

He nodded in agreement. We laid there for a few more

minutes, gazing at one another. It wasn't uncomfortable, just new. Before, if we were in a bed together, we were tangled together, but now there was an invisible wall. A barrier that kept our bodies' will at bay.

The effects of my medical cocktail began kicking in, and I let out a deep yawn.

"It's getting late," he noted, taking that as a cue. He stood and stretched, leaning down and kissing the top of my head. "Goodnight, Lila love."

I stared at him as he turned and walked to the doorway; my chest constricted at the thought of him leaving.

"Wait!" I called out to his retreating form, my hand reaching out to him. I couldn't stand to watch him walk away from me again. "Please," I said in a whisper. "Don't leave me."

He stopped in his tracks and turned toward me, his expression a combination of hopeful and frightened at the same time.

"I'm just going next door, Honeybear, to sleep in your guest room. I'll leave the door open so all you have to do is call for me, okay?"

Tears filled my eyes, my bottom lip quivering. I hurt, I was tired, and he was leaving.

Panic rose in his features at my distress. "Oh, no, please don't cry. I'm right here, baby, I'm right here." His hand reached out to stroke my hair.

I wasn't ready to forgive him, and I wasn't ready to let him back in, but I couldn't stand to not be near him. The other room was too far away.

Why couldn't the drugs take away the pain in my heart, as well?

AWOKE WARM AND IN PAIN, STRUGGLING TO GAIN A FULL BREATH. There was a squeeze around my chest constricting me even further. I opened my eyes and turned to find Nathan's closed ones in front of me. His arms were wrapped around me, our legs entangled. We had both drifted in the night, our bodies not fighting the pull as they crawled to find each other.

"Nate." I was quiet as I tried to rouse him. As much as I loved being wrapped in his arms, it hurt to breathe and my bladder was screaming at me, as well. "Nathan, I need to go to the bathroom."

My chest tightened over the fact I needed help doing such menial tasks, but I couldn't walk yet, even on crutches.

He made a cute noise before snuggling further, mumbling something I couldn't understand. "Nathan." I tried again, this time stroking his cheek, hoping my touch would stir him.

His eyes fluttered open and a lazy smile spread on his face. "Mmm, Honeybear." His voice was sleepy and he snuggled in again, his eyes closing.

His movement caused a surge of pain to shoot through my

chest. I drew in a sharp breath and cried out in pain, my eyes screwed tight.

That got his attention and his eyes shot open, staring at me in horror. "Oh, shit!" he exclaimed before releasing me. "I'm so sorry!"

His hands were frantic, but gentle, as he assessed me like adrenaline was running through him in his panicked search of my body. Mumbled apologies slipped from his lips, but I couldn't get him to look me in the eye so I could tell him to stop, that I was all right.

He ran into the bathroom and came out with the first aid kit. I twitched, wondering just what the hell he was planning on doing with it. Before I could even ask he left the room again, returning with a glass of water and a handful of my medication bottles.

It was past ridiculous. "Nate!" He jumped, startled at my reaction, his movements ceased. "What the hell are you doing?"

"Umm…you're hurt."

"I hurt anyway, but I cried out because you squeezed my ribs. Once you stopped, the pain lessened to its 'normal' level."

He stared at me, and I watched the wild look leave his eyes and his breathing calm. He kissed my forehead before returning the items he had gathered back to their rightful places.

After a bathroom break, he made up some breakfast, instant oatmeal, and we ate in the bed while watching the morning news. Once we were done eating, he returned our dishes to the kitchen and climbed back on the bed with me. We flipped through channels, settling on a marathon of some reality show.

We lay there, side by side, watching as they went through outbuildings and homes, yards and estates, searching for unknown hidden treasures. The entire time I felt Nathan's eyes on me, and every once in a while his fingers would gently run down my cheek, against my arm. Goose bumps formed and fire burned in the wake of his touch.

It was strange how comfortable I was with his touch in that moment even after everything that had happened between us. Was it because I finally knew without a doubt I was in love with him? I swallowed, and my eyes drifted to his hands on me. My heart fluttered and my skin warmed at his touch.

I wanted to launch myself at him, straddle his hips, and sink down on his perfect cock. His hands grabbing me, teeth biting my skin, the need I always felt pouring out of him. My body was desperate for the connection with him that I hadn't felt in almost a month.

A muscle twitch reminded me how such antics would not be good as pain shot down my leg. Also, my fears and insecurities about Nathan reared their ugly heads, and the feeling retreated. As much as I wanted the comfort of his body, we weren't ready for that yet.

After a few hours and a nap, Nathan turned to me with a mischievous grin.

"What?" I asked, knowing that face meant trouble.

He held up the *Jane Eyre* DVD. "The doctor cleared me; I'm all healed from my lobotomy. I'm more than happy to watch it with you."

I narrowed my eyes at him. "You know, it's a chick flick. You might need another lobotomy to get through it."

He smirked at me. "We'll see about that."

He got off the bed and popped the DVD in. There was a small buzz of excitement running through me. It always happened when I was about to watch it, but there was something different about watching it with Nathan, the man I loved.

I was surprised when an hour and a half later Nathan was still awake; in fact, he'd been enraptured by it.

Erin stopped by that afternoon to drop off some home-made enchiladas and stayed to play a board game with us. Something other than television was wonderful. I lost focus about halfway through and ended up napping through the remainder. Erin won, though Nathan was not convinced she played fair.

I woke up a while later to Erin sitting on the bed next to me. Her focus was on something in her lap. She was working with large needles in her hand, and yarn to her side: knitting.

"You know, Lila, I'm here for you if you need to talk. I'm hoping we can be friends, so I'm here not only for my idiot cousin, but for you." Her head rose and her eyes met mine. There was nothing false in her eyes; no acting. She was sincere and straightforward. No games, no gimmicks.

"Where's Nathan?" I asked.

"He had to run a few errands. It's just you and me." She smiled before her attention moved back to her project.

My mouth opened, and I spoke without meaning to. "I'm scared."

She looked back up and gave me a small smile, her fingers moved to brush a lock of hair behind my ear. "I know, sweetie. Baby steps. You *will* get through this. I know it's rough now, but you can lean on me for support—Nathan, George, Sarah, Teresa, Caroline, Andrew, Trent, and Darren—all of us. You're not alone anymore."

I froze at her last sentence. "What do you *know*, Erin?" Her brother-in-law was my therapist, and I knew about doctor-patient confidentiality, but I began to worry.

Her brow scrunched and she shook her head. "I don't

know anything. All I know is that Nathan said you have no family, besides Teresa and her husband."

I sighed in relief. I didn't like people knowing the hell I grew up in, because I couldn't stand the look of pity I always saw in their eyes. I got out, away from them; from *him*. I went to college, graduated from law school, and had a nice job. I had become something, even when most of the time I still felt like nothing.

I took a deep breath, a bad idea when my ribs cried out in protest. Erin's words and the sharp pain sparked a memory I was unable to stop from surfacing. It was sudden. I was lost.

My body shook as the memory of each hit, each kick, each pull of my hair, and each slap and punch to my face flashed into my mind. The snap and crunch of my broken bones and the painful breathing they created.

I was unguarded, the memory assaulting me, completely taking over my entire body and mind. I couldn't get free of it.

"Lila!" Nathan's voice called out, and I was back. "Are you okay? Talk to me."

Nathan was there. I didn't know when he'd returned, but his hands were holding either side of my face, his expression frightened and worried. I couldn't answer his question because I didn't know.

Then I noticed wetness from my tears streaming down my face. I glanced over to Erin and saw the fright in her eyes as well, tears also flowing freely down her cheeks.

I pulled Nathan closer, hiding my head in his neck while I tried to calm down. What had I said, what had I done, for Erin to wear that look?

It took a few minutes for me to settle, and I pulled away from his warm embrace. His thumbs brushed my tears away.

"So," I began, wanting to pull the attention away from me and whatever had happened. "What did you get?"

Nathan regarded me for a moment, checking to make sure I was really okay before grabbing the bags. "Well, I picked up a few television shows I thought you might like, as well as more movies. And I also picked up a Wii game system and about a dozen games to help keep you occupied. We can't keep watching Jane and Mr. Rochester." He winked at me.

I stared up at him in disbelief. "That's a lot of money. You already bought me a movie."

He shrugged his shoulders. "Something to keep you entertained, take your mind off things. Plus, it can be therapeutic."

I didn't buy his reasoning, but was happy to have something fun to do while bedridden. Nathan smiled like a kid on Christmas when I asked him about the games he bought. He was so excited, but competitiveness reared when Erin started trash talking him.

Nathan grumbled about Erin cheating on their last game, while a sly smile crept up on Erin's face. "He's a sore loser."

Nathan handed me my next dose of meds, and an hour later I was out again.

Nathan was still carrying on about Erin's cheating ways even hours later. She did not play fair during their game, and I was awoken by name calling and elbow jabbing. She did make fantastic enchiladas, though.

We spent all of Saturday and Sunday in my bed watching a myriad of movies Nathan picked up. He must have bought fifty movies to keep me occupied.

Teresa and Sarah made their motherly presence known on Sunday, bringing more food. It seemed they both thought I would starve to death in Nathan's care. Neither stayed very long, as both would be spending a lot of time with me during the week.

I watched as Nathan interacted with both his mom and Teresa. There was no pretense or act—just a guy talking with his mom.

He was joking around with them, mostly with his mom, about food and cooking. According to her, Nathan was not to be trusted in the kitchen, though I think he'd improved since the days of his mother's memory.

The entire time they were there, and even after, he was touching me: soft caresses and light squeezes. Small little gestures that added up to my being unable to deny what he wanted, which was to be close to me.

At one point, he threw his head back in laughter at something, and I stared in disbelief.

Nathan was a different man than he was before my accident. I began to believe his words that he was altered. He never complained about any of my requests or needs, but carried them out. He mentioned a newfound respect for his family in all they'd done for him in caring for me.

I awoke after a nap on Sunday curled into Nathan's side. I attempted to retreat, to separate us by rolling on my back. Pain shot through my ribs and my leg. I tried not to make a sound, but it was no use.

Nathan's eyes snapped open at my noise, and he sat up. His eyes locked onto the clock, then he jumped up from the bed and ran to the kitchen. He returned a short moment later with a fresh glass of water and my next dosage.

"Why didn't you wake me?"

"I was just repositioning. I was fine until then," I explained.

His fingers brushed my hair back. "I wish I didn't have to go to work tomorrow."

"Your mom and Teresa will be here. I'll be well taken care of," I said to reassure him. His brow scrunched, and I had the feeling he didn't like my answer.

We spent the remainder of the day playing a few games, nothing too exerting, and watching more movies.

The next morning the alarm went off, and I groaned as I attempted to silence it before realizing it was on Nathan's nightstand. He rose, picking up a groggy me on his way to the bathroom. I wasn't quite awake and nuzzled into his neck, my hand clenching his t-shirt. I might not have been with it, but he was correct in thinking I needed to use the facilities.

He returned me to the bed afterward and resumed getting ready while I fell back asleep. I felt his lips on my forehead a little later, along with the next dosage of meds. I was getting really tired of all the drugs, but I knew they were needed.

"My mom is running behind, so I'll stay until she arrives."

I shook my head. "I'll be perfectly fine until she gets here. You need to get to work." He grimaced. "Go."

He leaned over and kissed my forehead again. "If you need anything, just call, okay? I'll check in at lunch."

My gaze followed him as he walked out, and I sighed when I heard the door click. It was the first moment of peace I'd experienced since the morning of the accident. No beeping machines, no nurses, no people asking me if I needed anything. Just...*silence.*

My life had become a routine: wake up, take meds, watch a movie, eat, take meds, nap.

For days this trend continued, the only variation being who was assigned as my babysitter.

At first, it'd been difficult for me to rely on Sarah and Erin because I didn't know them. However, the more time we spent together, the closer we became. We became even closer in some more intimate ways when bathroom breaks came around and they had to help me with some embarrassing, private matters. They almost seemed happy to do it, almost as if it was proof I trusted them and was allowing them into my life.

Today they were staring at me, glints of mischief as they settled in.

"Why are you fighting this thing you have with Nate?" Erin asked. "I'm just curious, because I see the way you look at him."

I sighed and took a deep breath, as well as a leap of faith. "Because it's hard to fight for someone you never thought you deserved. Nathan is above me. He's gorgeous, much smarter than me, social. The only thing I have to offer is my body."

Erin and Sarah shared a look, a silent conversation before Erin turned to me.

"He told you everything, and you said you couldn't give it a real try? Why?" Erin asked. Her expression was almost as sad as Nathan's when I said it to him, but I couldn't figure out why she would have such an emotional response. I was also surprised by the way her voice sounded tight and was breaking a little.

"From what little I've heard, you all sing nothing but praise about Grace. I'll never be able to live up to that. I'll never be her. I'm me and I'm fucked up, and any delusions I once had that we could be something died the second I learned he was still in love with her."

I wiped away the tears that sprang to my eyes, not strong enough to pretend anymore. Sarah stood from her chair and walked over to my side of the bed, her arm wrapping around me.

"Oh, Lila," Sarah replied with a sigh. "You are very worthy of him."

Sarah looked up to Erin for support. Erin took a deep breath and began, "Nate has accepted her death, that she's gone, but he's never gotten over the guilt. Until he deals with that, he can't let her go from his heart. He blames himself for everything, and he can't stand the thought of the same thing happening to anyone else. He cut us all off. I hadn't seen him in months. Bad enough we lost Grace and the baby, but we also lost Nate."

Sarah sniffed, the conversation digging up painful memories. "Grace was a lovely woman, but you bring life and meaning to him. She struggled with the ability to let go and move on after each miscarriage, and Nathan never had a reason to move on after she died. Yes, he loved her, very much, but with you I see a spark I've never seen in him. Love has many shapes and depths, some richer than others. His for you is breathtaking."

Sarah's words gave me hope that maybe he could heal and let go; that we both could overcome our ghosts. There might not be white horses riding off into the sunset, but there could be happiness, and an all-consuming love.

The fact that his mother approved of me was monumental. Not since my own mother died had that been in my life. My heart warmed at the simple sight of her.

D R. MORGENSON WASN'T SOFT IN HANDLING US, DESPITE ALL that had happened. He made good on his threats from the outburst at the hospital, and now we were both in a more intensive therapy program than before.

We planned to meet twice a week; once would be an individual session, and the other would be a joint session. The individual sessions were to make sure we both got back on track after months away. He said the joint session was to help us understand each other better and to make sure we opened up and communicated.

The day of our first joint session came, and my stomach was fluttering with butterflies circling within, my nerves skyrocketing.

Nathan came into the bedroom in the early afternoon and picked me up to take me into the living room where Darren was waiting to start our session. It was decided that having our therapy in my home would be less of a strain on my mangled, healing body than trying to transport me back and forth to Darren's office. My stomach was in knots and a wave of nausea almost overcame me as we made our way.

We were going to talk and get everything out in the open. I was conflicted. A part of me wanted to be there for him, to know how best to help him, and I couldn't do that unless I knew what happened to him. But deep down inside, I was afraid. What if I really couldn't handle hearing about his pain and seeing him relive it just for me? I wasn't worth it. I knew that, but I was too selfish to let go. I needed him, so that included sharing the burden of his pain.

Even scarier than learning about his trauma was him hearing about mine. No one wanted me, I knew that, and Nathan's illusions of me, or what he thought was me, would evaporate into thin air. I'd be lost without him there to hold my hand.

It was the sole reason I was holding back, and it was a habit I had to stop. Darren told me if I continued on that path I'd lose my one shot at being happy, so I bit my lip and held my breath as we entered my living room.

Not a word was spoken as he sat me down on the chaise lounge on one end of the couch, taking care that my leg was supported, and yet my insides were clenching violently.

Nathan sat down next to me and gripped my hand in his, making it apparent he was feeling the exact same way.

"How are you both today?" Darren asked.

I blinked. Was it a trick question? Could he not see the expressions we both wore? I couldn't even look Nathan in the eye, but from my periphery it was obvious he wasn't handling this well already.

"Grand." Nathan's voice was curt, his eyes glaring, hackles up.

"I'm… Fuck, I don't know." I shook my head.

"I know this a little scary but—"

"Big fucking understatement, Doc," Nathan blurted out.

Darren chuckled. He understood. He knew us both. There was no guessing.

"Okay, so you're not happy to be here with me, I get that. Relax. We're all here to help each other, and you should consider me a friend, not a doctor to dissect you and break apart everything you say until you're internally bleeding." I released a breath I hadn't realized I was holding at his statement. Darren gave a kind smile in return. "I want you both to realize I will never allow you to leave our sessions if you're feeling upset. All you have to do is say you're not okay, and we won't stop until you're feeling better."

Nathan gave a tug at my hand and tucked my arm under his, pulling me closer in a protective manner. "I've done this before, couples counseling, and it's…not pleasant."

My brows shot up. He did this with Grace? I always had the impression they had a blissful marriage, so why couples therapy?

He turned to me a little and whispered, "When she kept miscarrying, we went through a rough patch, and I wasn't always as sensitive as I should have been."

I nodded and leaned into him to show my support.

"Nobody's here to blame anyone, Nathan. In fact, I don't even want you to think that word. Blame is a way of shifting unpleasant feelings. Feelings aren't right or wrong, they just are, and we can accept all feelings no matter what they are. Remember that. Feelings aren't wrong. If you can take that in, it will free you up. You'll be surprised at how liberating that one little motto can be."

Darren shifted his gaze to me next. "Do you remember what your biggest emotional reaction was when you were in the hospital a few weeks ago, before the accident?"

"Yes, I—"

He cut me off quickly. "I don't need you to tell me or re-live it for now. We'll get to that in time, but I want you to think about what happened afterward."

I nodded, even though I couldn't for the life of me remember what did happen, except that Darren was there for me after I freaked out about someone calling my dad.

"You can't remember very well, can you?"

"No." I shifted uncomfortably in my seat.

It was disconcerting to feel like someone else knew me better than I knew myself. He seemed to have an unfair advantage. Nathan looked puzzled.

"The reason you can't remember is because when you go into parataxic distortion, things become that—distorted. You can't think clearly, your emotions become the sole focus, and your head gets fuzzy. Memory is skewed and off. So, even if you do remember, you won't see it for what it was. You might see the person who offended you as monstrous, or hideous, or being out to get you, when that may not be accurate at all." He grabbed a file from his bag.

I swallowed hard. What had I said to him? I was nervous to think I might have been out of my ever-loving mind.

Darren smiled at me in a reassuring gesture. "I see here you fired one of the nurses and told her to get the hell out of your sight for even saying your father's first name."

I what?

My fingers felt ice cold, and so did my toes. It was like all my circulation was congregated in my chest. I had no recollection of that interaction at all.

He was waiting for a response, and I was hesitant. "I... don't remember that."

"It's okay. Sometimes our mind also blocks stuff out when we're in this mode. It's an act of self-preservation; to protect yourself."

"What does this have to do with anything?" Nathan asked, sounding frustrated.

"I'm pointing this out to both of you because your memories might be much worse than what actually happened."

"Fuck that and fuck y—" Nathan began, but was cut off by Darren's hand going up in a defensive gesture.

"I'm not trying to downplay what happened to either of you, just trying to help you gain a different perspective. At first, some people find it's easier to detach a little emotionally, to get some of their emotions out of the way. Once you've sorted through your shit, sorry for the slip, but after that, after you can lay it all out on the table, you then go back and figure out how you feel about all of it. Then you deal with it, but only after seeing the truth of what it was."

I remembered his parataxic distortion speech before. He was rehashing it but in a less detailed, lecturing manner.

"Nathan, when you hurt Lila on the day of the anniversary of your wife's death, you didn't mean to do that to her, did you?"

"Absolutely not. I was sick with myself when I realized what I'd done."

I ran soothing circles on Nathan's hand. There wasn't a doubt in my mind anymore that he hadn't meant to hurt me. I was never angry with what he did to me physically; it was the rejection that stung.

"And you didn't remember much of it because you were in a heightened level of distortion. Lila didn't realize you were in such a state, otherwise she might have treaded a bit lighter and not offered herself to you in that way." Darren cleared his throat. I could tell things were already going to head in an ugly direction. Bracing myself for the accusations, I shut my eyes and held them closed. "Lila, you need to hear this. Open your eyes, please."

I refused. The session was already hurting too much. I didn't think I could take hearing I was the reason Nathan was worse instead of better.

"I'm fine," Nathan whispered in my ear, like he was reading my mind.

I shook my head. "You're not fine. I made you do that. If I'd left you alone like you asked me to, we wouldn't even be here."

"Yes, we would. We need this, and that day wasn't the only problem. It was us being tipped over the edge we'd been clinging to by our fingertips. We are both far from okay, and if it led us here, then I'm sorry, but I'm almost glad it happened. For the first time in four years, I want to get better, I have a reason to get better. I want you to get better, too. I want to be with you."

I opened my eyes and felt a shift in the room. They were both looking at me, but it was different somehow. They didn't pity me, or coddle me. It was a look of adoration and appreciation, almost like they were confident I would get through this with flying colors. They made me feel brave, strong.

"Okay," I murmured. "I want to learn. What can I do to make things better?"

Darren's face split into a brilliant grin. "There's a lot you both can do to make this better. You both love each other, so that's the basis for all this. All we need is a few tools to keep things healthy and manageable so they don't fall apart on one or both of you when things get rough. And trust me, you both will have down days and it *will be* rough. To expect everything to be perfect would be setting you both up for failure."

Darren's soothing voice set me at ease and my jumpiness ratcheted down a notch or two.

"When you're grieving the loss of Grace or your child, your instinct is to bottle up and blame yourself. That has to stop. I know you don't want to talk about it to Lila, because you don't want her to be miserable and share your pain, but what about when she's feeling down about herself? Don't you want her to let you in?" Nathan nodded in agreement. "Then you have to do the same. It's about trust and friendship. I also know you lash out and then get physical."

Nathan inhaled in a rush, and a vein on his temple throbbed as he ground his teeth together loud enough I could hear it. He seemed to be holding his breath, as well.

"It's okay, Nathan. Sex is a part of your makeup as a man, and it's your way of feeling close to Lila, but it isn't fair of you to not tell her you're upset before you take her that way. It's obvious she wants to help you, and she has no problem giving herself to you to make you feel better, but it will help both of you much more if she understands it's an outlet for you, a form of therapy. A way to feel connected. It can be a tremendous help in healing you both, but it has to be done with respect, and that means telling the other partner you feel hurt or scared, and need them to reciprocate by being affectionate or sexual. You might even find it's some of the best sex you've ever had, even more so than makeup sex after a fight." Darren smiled with a warmth that reflected his respect and friendship with Nathan.

Nathan grinned, and I blushed. There was no arguing with that statement. It was some of the best sex when one of us was reaching out with our body to feel okay inside.

"After you're done connecting that way though, in order for it to help and be healing, you have to then talk about what you felt hurt about. I think you'll be amazed to find that after sex your head is clearer and you can make better sense of your feelings. You feel relaxed and trusting of your partner as you're lying there in each other's arms."

Nathan opened his mouth to speak but thought better of it and closed it. "I…that's when I feel the most open to speaking, but I know Lila's not always comfortable sharing what happened to her. I don't want to force her."

"You won't have to. If you open up first and make the first move to be vulnerable, you'll find Lila will do it on instinct. It's how this works. You give first, Nathan, because you left her, and you'll find she'll begin to trust you again." Darren looked at me to make sure I was okay. I hadn't realized a few tears had slipped down my cheeks.

I was desperate to believe Darren, but I was skeptical. Was it that easy?

Darren focused on me, his brow crinkled and there was a look of concern in his eyes. "What's going on? Can you tell me what you're thinking?"

"No one ever held me when I was sad or hurt. When Nathan does that after we've been in bed together, sometimes I feel worse, not better." I felt like shit for saying that, but I had to be honest if we were going to get anywhere.

Nathan's face fell. "I think I knew that." His grip loosened on my hand and began to pull away. I gripped it hard, to let him know this wasn't a rejection, and it was me begging for help.

"I don't know what to do about that. I want to change, I do, but this is who I am, who I've been for so long. I don't know any other way to be," I cried.

Darren stood up and gave me a patient look. "That's true; this is who you've become because you were forced into it. It was survival. But now, we've moved past survival. If Nathan promises you he won't leave you again, do you think you'd be more apt to not be afraid and to open up a little bit?"

"I suppose…" I didn't want to promise anything I couldn't deliver.

A few days after our session was my first follow-up appointment. The doctors said my progress was going well, and I was able to have my stitches removed. It would still be another week before I would be allowed to use the crutches and even then only part of the time to start. They wanted to make sure my bruised ribs were healed before I exerted myself too much.

While it had been Sarah who took me to the hospital for my appointment, it was Nathan who took me home. With prescriptions already digitally en route, we drove to the drugstore that wasn't far from our building.

"I'll be right back," he said as he pulled on the handle to open the door

"Wait, I can't go with you?"

I needed out and, damn it, and he was going to take me out. I'd been cooped up for weeks and suffering from a serious case of cabin fever.

"I'm just going in to pick up your meds; I'll be back in a minute."

With that he left me sitting alone in the car, staring at the brick wall in front of me. Fifteen minutes later, which had seemed like forever, Nathan returned. He was so tense he moved with almost a stiff limp. Instead of walking to the driver's side door, he opened mine.

I quirked my brow at him as he cursed under his breath. "They won't let me fucking sign for your meds."

It wasn't until he leaned into the car and his arms moved under my body did I understand. A smile broke out on my face.

Freedom!

Agitation seeped from him as he pulled me out, but he seemed to calm somewhat when my arms wrapped around his neck.

My eyes were happy to have more stimuli, and I was looking everywhere like a kid in a candy shop. I wanted him to let me down so I could explore, but I knew there was no way he would.

We walked up to the pharmacy counter, maneuvering past the small line of people. "Here she is."

I turned to look at the pharmacist who pushed the paper for me to sign. A quick signature and then Nathan shifted, juggling me a bit. He pulled out his wallet and I tried to protest, but was met with a glare, silencing me. After payment was made, he handed me the bag and turned to walk toward the door.

Hell no.

It was my first adventure out of the hospital or the house in nearly two weeks, and I was going to make damn sure I made it last.

I looked at him and said, "Hey, while we're here, there are a few things I need to pick up."

He turned to me. "Just give me a list; I'll pick them up for you later."

"But, we're already here," I argued.

He sighed. "I need to get you back to bed."

My jaw clenched. He was being difficult, and I was going to get my taste of freedom. I stared at him, our eyes locked in some silent battle.

"Put me down."

"Lila…"

"Put me the fuck down!"

He glared at me and took a deep breath. "You can't even stand."

"Fine, there's a motorized cart at the door; I saw it when we walked in."

Another silent argument with our eyes ensued before he relented with a huff. We were headed toward the door again, but just before, he detoured to the cart that was stationed there, plugged into the wall.

He sat me down, grumbling about needing to get me home. I'd been home for a week now; it wasn't going anywhere.

As soon as I was on the seat, my casted leg extended, I was off.

I raced away from my captor like a bat out of hell…or like a crippled lady on a scooter, but it was the imagery that counted. It took him two strides to catch up. After all, I was racing at about three miles per hour.

I started out aisle by aisle, adding things to the cart. I didn't even know or care what was going in, but I sure as hell was having fun.

Nathan wasn't. He was pissed, still limping by my side. The way he was hovering around me made him look like a Jack the Ripper stalking his next victim and less like a frustrated boyfriend with a disobedient girlfriend on wheels. Everyone who was in an aisle we were in would give him a rather large berth. They could tell he was a man who was having difficulties controlling his anger.

What I saw was a man who needed a nice long blow job to get all the tension out, but he'd have to deal with it. He could chase me around, cursing under his breath; it added to the freakish, hot sensuality he was exuding in that moment. That "I'm going to spank your ass red so you can never sit in a scooter again" vibe that was exciting me, but could not override my freedom fun.

He was furious, fists clenched at his side, and I could tell he wanted an outlet. It was amusing to play with him, so I laid it on thicker, smiling and waving at him like I was on parade. He growled. My smile turned to a glare. Spoilsport.

Almost everything I threw into the cart, Nathan pulled back out, arguing it wasn't something I needed.

I even tried tampons, but he grabbed the box and put it back on the shelf, reminding me I was on the shot and didn't have periods.

Damn him for remembering.

He continued to chase me around the store, reaching into the basket and plucking items back out. I would slap his hands, glaring up at him, but he just glared back. He was spoiling my fun. Then again, it was a fun game to have him chasing me… not that I'd tell him.

It was difficult not to smile and laugh at my newfound freedom as I zipped around. My hair was blowing in the breeze, and I caught a glimpse of myself in the mirrors near the ceiling. The image I portrayed could only be considered one of a mad woman, and in my giddy state that was almost how I felt.

After almost an hour, a very irate Nathan and I exited with two bags full of who knows what.

Nathan was fuming as he placed me back into the car, and

I tried to mirror his look, but was unsuccessful. He maneuvered around the outside of the car.

"Party pooper. No blow job or party favors for you," I said under my breath, giggling afterward. I followed him with my eyes, still pretending to glare at him. He needed to lighten up. Maybe I should have taken him for a spin on my lap around the store a few times on the fabulous freedom scooter? I stifled a roar of laughter at the thought.

God, I was losing it.

He slammed the driver's side door upon entering, not happy with how our excursion had gone. He was angry, and I couldn't keep the smile from my face, try as I might.

Then I couldn't keep my humor of the situation at bay.

Laughter, full and deep, sprung from me. My body shook from the force, despite the pain.

Nathan turned to look at me as if I'd gone mad. The more he watched me though, the more it began to dawn on him.

"You did that on purpose?" he asked through clenched teeth.

I couldn't speak; the giggles took full control, so I nodded. Nathan looked appalled, but my state became contagious and he joined in.

"You little…" he trailed off. "I can't believe you!"

"Freedom!" I cried out, my fist pumping in the air.

He smiled and shook his head, backing out of the space and heading home.

Score one point for Honeybear, and none for Jack the Ripper. Victory was sweet.

It was later that night as we were snuggled into bed, watching a movie, when Nathan's hand reached out to cup my face, his eyes beseeching. "Lila, I…I'll do anything to have you trust me again."

"Where did that come from?" I angled my head back to get a better look at him. Maybe my lunacy was spreading…

He sighed and tugged at the back of his neck. "I had a session with Darren, and I don't need him to tell me what to promise you. You already know, but I'm going to tell you until you believe it. I love you more than I've ever loved *anyone*."

My eyes went wide in shock. More than Grace and his baby? How could that be? That was a huge thing to say. And I… believed him.

"I have a reason to live again—*you*. I want us to be together from now on. Live together, have holidays and birthdays together. Hell, I'll go wherever you want me to go and do whatever you want, but I need you to trust and believe me first before we can—"

In a flash, my arms were around his neck, pulling him to me.

He was my whole world. He had been since that first night.

I was still wary, but with what he had admitted, how could I not try? Couldn't I try to let him in again, try to trust him? Could we start fresh, from the beginning?

I released him and lay back down, snuggling into my pillow. "Do you… You say you love me. Do you love me more than her? Really?"

His eyes widened in fear before softening. "Yes."

"Then why won't you let her go?" I asked, my voice breaking as a tear slid down my cheek.

THOUGHT NATHAN AND I WERE MAKING PROGRESS UNTIL THAT night when I asked him why he couldn't let go. It seemed he didn't like my question.

What was it they say? One step forward, two steps back? Well, that was what happened. Nathan began to withdraw the next day. The change was noticeable that morning; he stopped touching me. His little touches and kisses were gone, and I mourned the loss.

He hardly talked to me, and touching was relegated to when he had to help me. Of course, his withdrawal caused me to do the same. I couldn't count the amount of times I almost broke down crying in front of him. Maybe I should have. The times I almost lost control of my emotions, I brushed it off as being in pain and he dropped it, even though he knew my pain had lessened.

I couldn't tell him it was because he was breaking my heart—again.

My one sentence, one question, ruined any progress we had made. I hoped it would open him up, bring us back together, but instead it was ripping us apart.

He was choosing her; he didn't want to let her go. My heart was fracturing, the mending that had taken hold, coming undone. I was holding myself together with a frayed thread, and I wondered if I would be shattered beyond repair.

My condo felt like a strange place to be. It was foreign to me. I felt like an outsider in my own home. I wanted to scream at him to leave if he didn't want to be there, but I couldn't stand for him to go.

There was an invisible wall between us at night. He still slept in the bed with me, but there was no warmth.

It was strange being surrounded by people, and yet I had never felt so…alone.

My insurance company called with the estimation on my car; it was totaled. I had no idea when I was going to do it, but I had to buy a new one. Also, they suggested I contact a lawyer to go after the driver of the other vehicle for the car, compensation for the loss of work time, along with my mounting and future medical bills. In talking with the police, I found out the driver never even applied the brake before he collided with me. He hadn't seen the light because he was texting.

Being without a car was one of the many reasons, my injuries being the greatest, as to why Nathan would need to drive me to work upon my return.

Nathan offered to help me look for a new car as had Andrew. Though I thought Andrew won in the enthusiasm category; he was researching for days.

I was allowed to return to work at a reduced schedule, despite Nathan's protests that I should stay home for another week. I was happy to be getting out of the house and returning to some sort of schedule. I'd spent over a week at the hospital and two at home, and my case of cabin fever was worsened by Nathan's new despondent mood.

We both agreed it was plausible for Nathan to drive me in the morning as we lived in the same building, and I no longer had a car, therefore no one would be suspicious. Only a few days prior I was granted permission to start using the crutches, though it was restricted to use in my condo for the first week. My doctor didn't want me using them too much due to the exertion, which left me with the wheelchair to get around outside and at work.

On my first day back we pulled up to our office building, surrounded by a deafening silence and an awkward tension filling the air between us. It was broken as Nathan got out and brought me my wheelchair from the trunk. He opened my door and leaned in to pick me up, placing me in the chair.

"Are you okay?"

"Fine," I replied, and we made our way into the building.

We entered and headed toward the elevators. An uncomfortable silence seemed to follow and remain with us in the small space, and I began to wonder if he would ever talk to me again. The elevator pinged when we reached our floor, and Nathan pushed me out.

"Welcome back, Delilah!" Libby, the receptionist, greeted as we exited the elevator.

"Thanks, Libby." I waved as we rounded the corner. She was always such a sweetie.

"How are you feeling?"

"I'm going to head to the office," Nathan said, interrupting us.

"Okay. Thanks, Nathan." I turned my attention back to Libby.

Libby watched him walk away and smiled at me. "That was nice of him to bring you in."

"It is. Since I can't drive, and no longer have a car."

"Yeah, you should be thankful," a familiar voice sneered from behind me.

My jaw clenched as I remembered the Boob Squad. Oh, how I hadn't missed them.

"Very thankful," I said, trying hard to smile and not tell Jennifer to stick it where the sun didn't fucking shine. I'd had a shitty past couple days, and was happy to be back. She didn't want to mess with me—I was fresh off the loony bin.

"He's being nice to you, but I wouldn't let it get to your head. Nathan would have no interest in someone like you." Kelly looked down at me in disgust.

Try as I might to ignore her, I felt the sting. Her words were hitting a little too close to home.

"Someone like *me*? What is that supposed to mean?" I hoped my distaste was obvious in my expression. Someone who didn't have the fat removed from her thighs only to be deposited into her boobs? Or someone who used her brain for something other than housing an occasional hat? They probably couldn't go out into the sun anyway; it would fry their unholy she-devil skin.

Jennifer straightened, an evil little smile creeping up on her vile red lips. "Plain. You have little personality, okay in looks, nothing much to offer. Nathan is above you. He belongs with someone of his caliber. Someone like me."

"You're out of your league with him, so I wouldn't even think about it, if I were you," Tiffany added.

Even with their cruel words clawing at my insides, it was difficult to keep my laughter at bay from their comments.

Nathan wouldn't touch them with a ten foot pole. "He's been here for almost six months, if he wanted you in the least bit, he would have gone after you by now."

Tiffany took on the same stance as Jennifer, joining in her upturned nose and assumed entitlement. "It's because of the fraternization rule."

I snapped, glaring up at them and their stupidity. "Fuck the fraternization rule. If a guy really wants you, that's what he'd say. He hasn't said it, hasn't approached you. He doesn't want you. Why don't you leave him alone and quit barging in while we are trying to work? It's obvious your flirtations are unnoticed and unwanted." Wanting to throw more salt in the wound and also take a jab at Nathan I added, "Maybe he's gay. Or maybe silicone doesn't appeal to him? I've heard he doesn't like plastic people. Either way—sounds like neither of you are on his radar."

The heat of their death glares had me smiling in victory as my savior arrived.

"Hey, Delilah. Welcome back. Ready to get the show on the road?" Owen asked, interrupting our little chat. It was a good thing too, because Jennifer looked like she wanted to deck me.

Yes, hit the wheelchair-bound woman. That sounds like a great idea. I'd love to see you fired.

Owen took hold of the chair and pushed his way past the Boob Squad. Their glares were burning a hole in the back of my head as we went.

"Nice going. Though, they'll be screaming about you later."

"Screw them. I've had a really shitty month, and I don't see why I should put up with their fucking high school bullying ways," I seethed. My blood pressure was rising, creating a throbbing in my leg. "I hope a stray dart punctures one of their silicone breasts to give them something truly upsetting to worry their small brains about, then they can forget I'm even here."

Owen and I settled down at my desk, I avoided Nathan, and went over what Owen had been doing in my stead. He had a few questions and a few items that needed some work, but all in all he was doing a very good job. I could see him getting the job full-time if Nathan or I ever left.

The mountains were still there, as to be expected, but at least the files hadn't grown too much with my absence and Nathan's reduced hours.

Andrew came in right at noon to take me home, interrupting Owen and I as we worked on a more intricate case. Nathan and Andrew shared a look; I wasn't quite sure if they were back to being okay with one another or not.

"Ready, Lila?"

I yawned and nodded. I hadn't expected how much being at work for only a few hours would affect me, but I was really tired.

I waved at Nathan and Owen as Andrew wheeled me away. "See you guys later."

Over the next few days, it felt like I was seeing Andrew more than Nathan. He decided to take the afternoon off; we went to the movies and grabbed some dinner. I let Nathan know, of course. I needed to get out, and that was difficult with Nathan. Between his mood, his control issues, and our need to hide our…relationship, or whatever you would call us, we couldn't go out together. So, I felt guilty, but I was also happy as a lark to be out of my condo.

I knew Nathan wasn't thrilled I was spending so much time with Andrew, but I was so restless and it provided me a much needed lifeline. It was more than that; Nathan wasn't fun to be around as of late. Spending time with him made me sad as I watched the rift between us grow, unable to stop it. After all the progress, there we were, back to square one. Only this time, there was no sex. Square zero, if there was such a thing. Strangers who were anything but strangers. Nathan knew me better than anyone. *Anyone.*

That was why his behavior hurt so much. Why I needed an escape and turned to the person who knew me second best, besides Caroline.

"Why are you so…sullen lately?" Andrew asked on the drive home. "I mean, he fucked up, but I thought you'd be, I don't know, happy to have him back. Am I wrong in the way I'm reading things here?"

I shook my head. "Things are…things are complicated."

"Complicated, how? Haven't you had it out?"

Tears welled in my eyes. "He… I don't know…" The tears began to stream down my cheeks.

"Hey, hey." Andrew pulled the car over and reached toward me, his thumbs brushing away my tears. "Tell me."

It all came pouring out: my insecurities, my loneliness, Nathan's distance.

"If he doesn't want to take care of you, let me. I'll take care of you."

"Thanks, Drew. I just…need to find out what's going on."

I cried on his shoulder the remainder of the way home.

Nathan had me crying, something I hadn't done in almost

ten years until I met him. The first time tears came to my eyes was when I saw his scars, because I could only imagine what he had gone through to get them.

Andrew dropped me off after our movie/dinner outing and had me laughing about something as we entered my condo, Nathan glared at us. The laughter stopped and my chest tightened as I tried not to believe the feelings he was evoking in me, but I couldn't stop them.

I thought about what Andrew said that night and decided to approach Nathan about his idea. I wasn't sure how I felt about it, having Andrew stay and help me with everything, but being with Nathan every moment throughout the evening was killing me inside.

"You know, Andrew…Andrew offered to take over tonight if you wanted a night off." I struggled to get the words out, my fingers twisting in my lap.

Nathan's eyes grew wide, and he turned to look at me. I didn't think I'd grown a second head, but by the expression he held, I was wondering where the closest mirror was so I could check.

"Out of the question," he growled through clenched teeth.

"Well, that's fine. It was just an offer. I'll be on my way." Andrew leaned down to kiss my cheek and give my shoulder a squeeze.

"Thanks, Drew."

Nathan was livid, based on the expression on his face.

I watched as Andrew left, somewhat afraid to look at Nathan. Still, my eyes found him, and he was staring at me in silence.

He stood and paced, his head snapping to look at me, his mouth opening as if to say something but no words came out.

After a few rounds of this, he turned and stood in front of me, his chest heaving as he glared down at me in utter disgust.

He clenched his fists and put them at the sides of his head, squeezing his eyes shut. He was reaching his boiling point.

He didn't say a word, merely opened his eyes, which were black with ire, then turned and left, slamming the door behind him. The damn crying picked up again, and I was sobbing into my hands.

He didn't want me in any way anymore. I'd fucked everything up. *Again.*

I called Caroline a few minutes later in a blubbering mess, unable to control all the emotions flooding from me. Being the good friend she was, she rushed right over.

I needed to learn how to be a better friend.

When she arrived, I told her what had happened and a little bit about Nathan's change, but she pressed me to tell her every last depressing detail. She then helped me change into something to sleep in, and onto the bed and under the covers.

My chest, which had been relatively quiet throughout the week, was now angry. Caroline laid me down on the bed, stroking my hair, as I settled.

A few hours passed when we heard him return, his body still visibly tense and more so when he saw Caroline. White powder clung to his hair and body, and I knew where he'd been and what he'd done.

There were more holes in his walls. He was going to hurt himself soon if he kept handling his anger that way. But what could I do?

Caroline pursed her lips and stood, arms crossed over her chest. "Can I speak to you for a moment?"

They walked outside the bedroom and shut the door.

Muffled yelling filtered in, a word here, a word there, but not much I could distinguish. A few minutes later, they walked in, Caroline sitting on the edge near my head, her fingers stroking at my hair line.

"Lila, I think he needs to leave," Caroline said. I nodded, unable to look at him. "I've got her. Get out."

"If that's what you want, Lila." His voice resigned.

I stared at the ceiling. I didn't stop him. He needed to figure things out for himself as I wouldn't be offering up my body as sacrifice to his anger. Better if a wall didn't survive the night than me.

"**O**KAY," DARREN BEGAN, HIS GAZE HARD AS HE LOOKED between the two of us. "Will someone tell me what has happened over the last week that caused this?" His hand motioned between the two of us, pointing out the obvious rift.

I lost it. All of the emotions I'd been holding back from Nathan's view came flooding out. I sobbed into my hands, and it was the first time in almost a week Nathan touched me. His fingers brushed against my arm before he drew back. The motion only made me sob harder.

"What the hell was that, Nathan?" Dr. Morgenson asked in annoyance.

"He doesn't want me!" I cried, removing my hands from my eyes. "I asked him why he couldn't let her go, and ever since then, he's ignored me! He doesn't talk to me, he doesn't touch me. He's angry all the time and looks at me with disgust. I want to tell him to leave then, if he doesn't want to be here... but...I..."

A new wave of sobs took over my entire body, and I began

to wonder what the hell was wrong with me. I'd never cried like that. Ever. Crying gave them power over me, and Nathan already had more than enough.

Darren was staring at me, shocked. His head moved to look at Nathan, and the surprise was evident on his face; I couldn't help but look, as well. In a tentative motion my head turned, and I saw the utter look of pain and horror etched into Nathan's features.

He jumped up from his spot on the couch and began pacing, his hands pulling against his neck. "I felt it was unfair! I was thinking of you." His movements became erratic as he paced. His fists clenched and unclenched, and I knew he was looking for a wall to punch. "I kept hurting you! Every time I touched you…and then I knew you were wondering if I wished you were her. I can't take this anymore, Lila!"

He looked tired, defeated, and more worn than I'd ever seen.

"You're right, Darren's right, my mother's right…none of it is fair to you. I'm trying to figure it all out, because what I want most of all is you, and I know we can't be together until I let go. Let go of her, let go of my guilt. I…I don't want to hurt you anymore. I can't do anything right!"

Darren shook his head and leaned back into his chair. "What did I say last time? You need to communicate! This hurt, confusion, pain, could have all been prevented if you had told her. Lila put herself out there, became vulnerable, and you pushed her away. All that we talked about, opening up, sharing; you threw it out the window."

"Dr. Morgenson?" My voice shook and was so timid, I wondered if he even heard me.

"I'm sorry, Lila. I…he's like family, and I let my personal

feelings overrule me for a moment," he said then turned back to Nathan. "If you're not ready to move on with Lila, there are plenty of men that would be honored to have her, and it's not fair for you to deprive her of the opportunity to have a full and happy life."

That stopped Nathan dead in his pacing tracks. He shot Darren a death glare, not fazing him in the least. "Not going to fucking happen."

"Fine, then start talking."

Nathan turned to me and began to lash out. "What the fuck was going on with you and Andrew this week?"

His question and attitude pissed me off. "What do you care? You won't even talk to me. You're pulling away."

"Why would…how could you even think that? I'm here for you every single fucking day!"

I shook my head as I spoke. "Maybe you are here in a physical presence, but mentally you've flown the coop. You built yet another fucking wall between us. It's like it was in the beginning, but this time I'm not getting anything at all from you!"

"Things were getting better and then you dropped that on me and I… What can I fucking do? Because I can't seem to do anything right."

"You were doing everything right. Then you became detached, empty."

Nathan sighed in defeat, slumping back down on the couch. "I'm always lost in thought. Trying to remember, trying to forget."

"Good, now you're communicating," Darren said, taking over the conversation. "Nathan, let's talk about your relationship with Grace." Nathan tensed beside me, clearly uncomfortable where he was heading. "Grace spent quite a bit of time on my couch the last few years of her life. I want to talk about why."

"Because we fucking lost four babies, that's why."

"You don't remember the toll your job placed on your relationship? You were hardly home."

Nathan's brow scrunched as he tried to remember. I could tell he was searching his memory to recall the bad along with the good he remembered with ease.

"Things weren't perfect, but I loved my wife. Sure, we had fights, like any other married couple. My wife knew my job was important to me. She knew it would take me away from her and our family for long periods of time. I tried to give my wife what she needed: a nice home, nice car...a baby. It's not my fault she couldn't..." he trailed off, and I watched as he froze.

I could see him working through the thoughts that assaulted him. He stood and began to walk away.

"Where are you going?" Darren asked him.

"Air. I need air." His fist was grabbing at his chest. His anxiety and panic was infectious as it rolled off him.

"You blamed Grace in some way for being unable to carry your child. Did you know you told me that in a session once?" Darren asked. Nathan stopped, his feet glued to his spot. "You used work to escape your guilt and the anger you felt toward her, the miscarriages."

"I loved my wife, and now she's dead because of me! I still love her. I love my little boy and all the others we lost so early on."

I knew Nathan would always love her, and I would never ask him to forget about her. That being said, it still stung when he so adamantly called out he loved her in the present tense.

"Each of them is a weight on your shoulders." Darren's

sympathetic tone suggested he knew it was Nathan's greatest hurdle.

Nathan's fingers tangled into his shirt at his stomach. "They were my responsibility and I…I failed them!"

It tore at my heart to see him so distraught. But like everything else about him, his agony was staggering in its strength.

"I'm hearing a reoccurring theme here. You keep referring to Grace as 'my wife.' Isn't that a bit unfair to Lila? Shouldn't she hold the top spot? You refer to her as 'your Lila' but not 'my girlfriend.' Curious, is there a reason behind that? Do you want Lila to be your wife?"

I scrunched my brow and looked up at Nathan who was staring wide-eyed at Darren.

"Hmm, that's interesting," he mumbled to himself and scribbled on his note pad.

I didn't know what he saw in Nathan's look, but the smile on Darren's face reassured me it was good.

"Why?" I asked for both me and Nathan, wondering what Darren saw in his reaction.

"How would you feel if Lila compared you to Andrew every day? Told you how she loves him? The times they shared together? How he was there for her when she had no one? How he cared for her and nurtured her?"

Nathan's whole body tensed at his words. "I would fucking loathe it; I wouldn't be able to deal with it."

"My point."

Recognition dawned in Nathan's eyes. Darren made Nathan start referring to Grace by her name instead of "my wife." He didn't want to be harsh about it, but it came across that way when he explained they had promised till death do we part and she was, in fact, dead. He continued that Nathan was holding on by doing this, and it could be hurtful to "his" Lila if it continued.

Darren moved on to Nathan's constant companion; his fear of the Marconi. Not for him, but for those he loved, myself included.

"I'm so fucking scared. I can't let them hurt any of you. If Lila, or Erin and Trent, or my parents, Alec and Brennan… I couldn't take it. I don't want anyone else hurt because of me."

Darren nodded. "This anxiety you have, I know it's based on real threats to you, but the problem is you are letting it rule your life and your future."

"How can I let go knowing they'll always be watching me? How do I let go and move on, let Lila be anywhere near me, knowing that?" Nathan asked. I reached out and slipped my hand in his. He gave a light squeeze.

"It's her decision."

Nathan's anxiety was rising again. The whole session had been such a push and pull, Nathan kept struggling, building walls and breaking them down at the same time and so fast I was having trouble keeping up.

"It's the things my dreams and nightmares are made of."

"Why is that?" Darren asked.

"Because, they're always of her. My dreams turn to poison. Wonderful visions, happiness, which turns to terror."

"We'll work on that. It will get better, but it's going to take some time."

Then Dr. Morgenson's gaze turned to me, and I felt the knots twisting in my stomach. My turn.

"You need to voice yourself. Your opinions and feelings do matter, Lila. You need to tell him what's bothering you. How do you feel? How did Nathan's pulling away affect you? Did his actions trigger anything?"

I didn't like that the attention had shifted to me, but what choice did I have? It wasn't only about me; it was about us. I braced myself, unsure of what might come flooding out.

"What part of your past is still haunting you and won't let you move forward?"

I froze as the words spun around in my head. My whole body tensed, and I shrank down into the couch.

"Stop," Nathan whispered into my ear. He was staring down at me, anger burning in his eyes.

"The words," I said, my eyes locked on Nathan's. "Over and over and over. Telling me how worthless I am. Telling me how no one will ever want me."

"What about physically?" Darren asked.

I flinched.

"She had some sort of episode the other day."

I turned to Nathan. "Will you tell me what happened?"

Nathan looked away, his jaw clenching in aggravation. "I can't help but wonder how often that happens to you when no one is around."

"What happened to Lila?" Dr. Morgenson asked.

Nathan shook his head. "I don't know. I came home to find Erin trying to shake her awake. She was screaming, blocking her face from some invisible attacker."

"What was she saying?"

I didn't want to hear. I didn't want to know. But I knew I needed to.

"She was begging for someone to stop. 'Please, stop, please. I won't tell, please stop,'" he recounted, anguish and anger in his expression, tears filling his eyes. "I didn't know what to do.

I'd never seen her like that, so unresponsive. It was like she was in her own world."

Tears pricked my eyes. Without speaking I pulled Nathan's hand to my left side and watched his eyes widen in remembrance of the conversation we'd once had. I then passed his hand over my forearm, near my wrist, then my hand, and finally my pinky finger that was crooked compared to the others.

"I had a concussion, as well. They waited until I passed out to take me to the hospital where they told the doctor that 'clumsy Lila' fell out in the woods onto some rocks. I told the doctor that wasn't right, but they said I wasn't remembering correctly due to the concussion. They waved it off, believing my father's recount. The bruises to show different didn't form until later that day."

I locked down my emotions; I had to if I was going to get through telling them. "I got a few slaps for that when we got home. Two days later I started researching how to get away. I couldn't live with them anymore. I had to get out. I called Joan a few days later and explained my situation. She believed me, and I was pulled from the house the next day while the investigation took place. By then the bruises had formed and faded a bit, but his hand prints were still visible and were entered in as evidence."

"What happened next?" Darren asked, pushing me further than ever before.

My hand moved around to my neck, where the deepest bruises had been. "The judge believed us, after seeing my injuries and the pictures. When they removed me, I went to stay with Teresa and Armando. Teresa was so kind, she worked with me. She never rushed and she helped me to recover. She made sure I ate anywhere from three to five times a day when the doctor said I was too underweight. I weighed a whooping eighty-seven pounds when I moved in with them."

My eyes were unfocused as it poured out. "I never smiled, and I shied away from Noah, the boy with a situation similar to mine. He was the same build and hair color as Adam. I hated that I categorized him in the same place in my mind as Adam, because he was so nice, but he understood. We became good friends, but before that happened he learned how to approach me, making it easier for me to distinguish the difference. Armando...it took us some time. He had a bald spot, so he kept his hair shaved off. Teresa got it out of me one day, and Armando stopped shaving his head that day. He wasn't as affectionate as Teresa, but he had his own way."

"How long were you with them?"

"After seeing the healthy changes in me, the judge separated me from my family and put me in the custody of Teresa and Armando. My family was not to contact me at all; a restraining order was placed on them."

I stared down at the floor, thinking about that time in my life, tears falling from my eyes, when I felt Nathan's hands on me. His strong arms pulled me into his lap and wrapped around me, his head buried in my neck. His body shook, and I ran my hands through his hair in an attempt to soothe him back.

"I'm not much, but I'm all yours," Nathan said, breaking the silence. "Everything that I am. I know I'll fuck up, but I promise you will never feel unloved or unwanted ever again."

"You can't promise that. Not after what you've put me through all week." I tried not to start bawling again, my bottom lip trembling.

His lips brushed against my neck. "Maybe not, but I will work damn hard to make it the truth."

We stayed in our little bubble, connecting for the first time in days, and I almost felt…whole.

"I must say, Lila, I'm quite impressed by how much you just opened up. I'm also quite proud because that is something you'd only hinted at in our past sessions." Darren's words pulled our attention away from one another and put it back on him.

"We're going to do a little experiment. I'm going to leave the room. Nathan, you're going to kiss her and show her with your body how much you worship and adore her. And when she feels safe, you tell her something she doesn't already know about you. Something about Grace, or the baby, or about your fears." Darren turned to me. "After he's done that, I want you think about how you feel. If it feels right, share something with him. If it doesn't, then show him with your body how you feel about him, and don't worry about your past for a few moments. He needs to know you love him."

Nathan nodded. "I do need to know that, so much." His tone was heartbreaking, and I felt on the verge of a yet another crying jag.

"And, Nathan, Lila needs your reassurance and your affections."

He left the room, and I waited, unsure of how to proceed. Was it going to be awkward to kiss and hug under our therapist's direction?

"Lila, I'll say it again. I will do anything to have you trust me again."

My breath stuck in my throat. He wasn't doing what Darren asked. He wasn't kissing me or hugging me. But it was what I needed to hear before I could allow him to touch me. What Darren didn't know was Nathan could read me. He knew what I had to have to feel secure in him.

"I'm beyond sorry for making you feel even the slightest bit as if I didn't want you this past week. It was never my intention. I got caught up inside my own head. I love you, so much. I want to make this all work, but I'm also so scared of what could happen to you by being with me. I don't want it to rule my life's decisions and feelings any longer. I want us together; I want us happy and healthy. No more masks, just Lila and Nathan."

Darren may have been wrong about how he instructed Nathan, but he was absolutely right about me. I didn't have the words, but my mouth needed to show him what he meant to me. So, I kissed him for all I was worth.

He responded, moaning into the kiss. The invisible wall we had put between us was gone for the moment.

No one seemed embarrassed when Darren returned, and he didn't ask for details. "Feel better?"

Nathan smiled. "Much."

"Emotionally we all feel like children at times. I have a little trick I do with families who come to me with kids. I tell the child when they feel sick inside or hurt to say a few simple words to their parents. Want to know what it is?"

"Yes." I was sitting on the edge of my seat like he held the magic answer to my problems.

"I tell them to say to their parent, 'I need lovey hugs' and then their parent has to give it to them no questions asked. It's a safe zone where they can get love before they figure out what the problem is. You can't open up to each other if you're scared. Trust has to be established first." He smiled with a kindness that made me feel reverent and almost idolize Dr. Morgenson in that moment.

"You don't have to use those particular words since they're very simple and childlike, but maybe you could find your own keywords together, to let the other person know it's important they drop what they're doing and give you some physical affection. But afterward, like with sex, you have to share something about why you needed it. Otherwise the person who gave it will feel rejected. Make sense?"

It seemed a steep price to pay, but I was willing to try it, so I agreed.

We ended the session by talking about what we needed to tackle on our next couple's session. Nathan seemed calmed, relaxed. I felt a little torn; I wanted to believe we'd made progress, but anxious and worried this wouldn't work.

But I was willing to try.

For him.

For *us*.

WHEN WE RETURNED HOME THAT EVENING, IT WAS WITH held hands and tiny caresses. We were reconnecting. It seemed as if the pieces of our puzzle were locking into place. Each day, each session, was a struggle, but one we came out of a little bit stronger and closer.

After our talk with Dr. Morgenson, things improved between us. Nathan's affections retuned and he was talking to me, and in doing so I began to talk to him. Deep conversations, the façades stripped away, leaving us exposed.

Dr. Morgenson was right; Nathan opening up caused me to open up naturally. It was painful, exposing the deepest parts of our fears and past heartaches, but at the end of the conversations we both agreed we felt a bit lighter, even though Nathan was feeling hostile toward my former family.

I told Nathan more about my father and Cheryl and how, all the way up until I was taken from their custody, I had hoped, a foolish hope, that somewhere inside his darkened soul, my father did love me. It's the want of any child, to be loved by their parents. I always told myself he was my father, and there had to be some part of him that cared about me.

That went out the window on the day the ruling came down and he tried to smack me, screaming hateful words and causing the bailiff to intervene.

I clutched onto Joan's suit as she formed a wall between my father and I, while the bailiffs attempted to restrain him.

"You ungrateful little bitch! This is how you repay me for being a burden? Look at what you've done! I never wanted you! I wish you'd never been born!"

"Mr. Palmer, you will get a hold of yourself!" the judge yelled, but my dad continued to come at me, nothing but anger and contempt in his features.

"You are nothing. You hear me? Nothing! You will always be nothing, just like she was. No one will ever want you!"

"I want you," Nathan's soothing voice called to me. "Come back to me, baby."

I blinked and took a moment to shake off the memory that had taken over. It felt so real; I was trembling and a little cold.

That was the last time I'd seen either of them. They were out of my life, but I wondered if I would ever be rid of them emotionally. At times it didn't seem they'd ever go away forever.

I took a deep breath; it helped to clear my head. When I looked up, Dr. Morgenson gave me an affectionate smile. "I must say, I'm very pleased at the progress you're making. Over the last few weeks you've opened up, told us about your family. You're learning how to express your traumatic past in a positive manner. This would indicate a real healing step in the right direction to your long-term emotional well-being."

Nathan leaned down to place a kiss on my forehead. "Good job, Honeybear."

Darren smiled at us and then continued on, "You may have more memories triggered similar to what you just experienced after you've been through a heavy session like today. However, after seeing the way Nathan handled it a few moments ago—I'm confident you'll be fine if it happens outside my office, or make-shift office as the case may be. This is a huge hurdle you've both jumped over. You're obviously in very good, capable hands."

What did that mean? If things hadn't gone well in his presence I'd be hospitalized again or put on more medication? I held my breath for a second and looked at Nathan beside me.

He stroked across my back and shoulders, his eyes soft.

"It's made Nathan angry though," I said. "The more I tell him, the more things he destroys. Soon there won't be any walls left in his condo. I don't want him to get hurt."

"Because if I ever see any of them again, they *will* be checking into the fucking hospital." Nathan fumed, his hands leaving me and forming into fists, clenching at his sides.

I reached for his hand to soothe him, but he pulled away, jumping up from his position on the couch. His agitation vibrated from his whole being; it was almost a palpable force in the room.

Even though his anger was intimidating and almost frightening with the speed in which he moved from sympathetic to livid, it made me love him all the more, because it was all for me. He was angry *for* me. I'd never had anyone that passionate about protecting and keeping me happy and safe. Even Teresa wasn't that intense about it, and she actually met and saw how awful my father treated me.

"No, Lila! You never did anything wrong! You were a child! It was his responsibility to take care of you. I can't fucking stand that they did all that to you. Especially that sack of shit you once called a brother."

"I think what Lila is saying is you need an outlet for your anger," Dr. Morgenson said. "It's not wrong to be upset about what happened and have harsh feelings toward her family, but I have to agree with her. It would do you good, so it doesn't stay pent up and you end up lashing out in harmful ways."

"If he does, then all the drywall manufacturers would be out of business." I smiled and let out a little chuckle.

When I looked up, Darren and Nathan were staring at me. Darren blinked and Nathan tilted his head, while I became self-aware and embarrassed. I was receiving that extra head look again.

Their strange looks melted into smiles and both were having trouble holding back their laughter.

It was a good laugh, and I found myself joining in.

To add to all the therapy, we now had special assignments. Nathan was enrolled in boxing and mixed martial arts to have a positive outlet for his anger and was to go twice a week. Darren said he needed to learn how to channel his explosiveness.

My assignment was to find a hobby. He suggested I try the local arts institute that held classes for adults. I needed a focus besides work and Nathan. It also forced me to be social and meet new people. Though I wouldn't be able to start for a couple weeks due to my limited mobility, I went online and signed up for the next round of painting.

I didn't know if I'd be any good at it, but at that point I needed something else to focus on. Not to mention it was a positive way for me to become more…normal.

A week later we were lying in bed, and watching some crap movie Nathan had put on. Even he was complaining. He kept repeating "movie bad" over and over.

This was out new ritual since I was still pretty much bed bound. I was getting a lot better, my lungs were healed up, and my bruises had faded away. We would eat dinner, something his mom or Teresa left, so all Nathan needed to do was heat it up, and then retire to the bedroom. After dinner we would surf the On Demand from my cage…I mean bedroom…and pick out a movie or two.

I couldn't wait to be free and mobile again, rid of my damn cast.

That night's pick was by far the worst. Some alien invasion in L.A. I'd never seen so much drama in what looked like an action movie.

After a while I snapped, and couldn't take anymore. "All right, that's it. Give me the remote. I'm tired of Movie Bad." I gave a little inward chuckle at the appropriate name I'd given it.

"There's only thirty minutes left." His eyes were still glued to the screen, watching the train wreck.

"Yes, and I've already lost over an hour of my life and countless brain cells. I'd like to keep from losing any more of either. I never got that lobotomy, remember? I want to keep my brain intact." I switched to demanding, holding my hand out. "Remote."

He smirked and held it out. I reached to grab it, but he pulled it away.

"Nathan."

"Delilah." He rolled his eyes and moved the remote in my direction. When my fingers touched the plastic, he pulled it from me again.

"Really?" I said with a huff.

He gave me his best sexy smirk. I figured out I was going to need a distraction to get what I wanted.

My eyes flickered to the TV and grew wide. "Oh, my God, what is that thing doing to her?"

It was enough. Nathans's eyes snapped back to the screen to see whatever it was I seemed so curious about.

"Ah ha! Mine!" I cried out in victory as I snatched the remote from beside him.

"No! I need to know what happens!" He whined, his attention turned back to me.

"I need my brain cells! Thinking good. Movie bad. Remote mine," I said like a cavewoman, and stuck my tongue out at him.

He lunged for the remote, landing across my body as I stretched it as far away as I could.

"Give me!"

"Never!"

We were laughing like maniacs as we played our game of keep away. He cheated and began tickling my sides. I was writhing beneath him, doing my best to get away from his fingers, as well as keep the remote from his grasp.

Our eyes locked, and our laughter died down. With the position we were in, him nestled between my thighs, the sparks between us ignited. All at once his lips crashed to mine, his tongue seeking, lapping at my lips, begging for entrance that I readily gave. I wrapped my arms around his shoulders, pulling him closer.

It was frantic and needy, composed of almost two months of repressed desire. His hands slid down to my ass, grabbing hard. He pulled my hips to his while he pushed his hard cock against my clit. I moaned against his mouth, my hands tangling in his hair, nails scratching at his neck. His lips moved down my jaw, kissing and nipping until he reached my neck. Teeth scraped against my skin, and I rocked my hips against his. He growled in appreciation before his teeth dug into the flesh of my neck, sending a fire roaring straight between my thighs.

My back arched off the bed and a loud, throaty moan escaped my lips. He was driving me wild, and I was in desperate need of him.

My moan had unfortunate consequences, cutting through the lust fog of Nathan's brain and all movement stopped.

He released me and jumped off the bed, pacing as he pulled at his neck. Never a good sign.

"Shit, shit, fuck! I'm sorry. I...I said I wouldn't until you said yes. I just got caught up in the moment."

My voice was soft as I reassured him. "It's okay."

He shook his head. "No, it's not."

"Yes, it is."

"I'm sorry, I...I need a moment," he said, heading to the bedroom door. "I'll be on the balcony. Yell if you need something." He gave me a reassuring smile. "I've been bad, I need a time out."

He headed out the door, and an ache in my chest began to grow. I tried to wave it off since I knew he was still in my condo and close by. He hadn't headed back to his place where he could smash his fist through walls again. Progress, it seemed, was finally happening.

My attention moved back to the TV, and I grabbed the remote, moving away from movie bad. I flipped through channels for about a half hour when he returned.

He smelled of cigarettes as he climbed onto the bed. It'd

been a while since he'd smoked, but I knew he did it when stressed and upset. The smell had me craving for one.

Strange how different our lives were from a few months ago. It was Friday night, and usually we were at the bar, drinking, smoking, and trying to forget everything that was wrong with us, taking comfort in each other's bodies.

We didn't talk about what happened; we were both there, we knew.

We didn't touch the rest of the night; though I did see his fingers twitch toward me more than once.

Nathan's normal casual caresses and kisses had died down a bit in the days to follow, but picked up once he felt he was safe, in control of himself again.

I, on the other hand, couldn't stop the wetness that gathered or the fantasies that sprung up from nowhere. Somehow, my body had forgotten what his felt like. Now that I had a small taste, the spark was reignited and my body craved him to the point of insanity.

It was very difficult to find any alone time since he was always around. I was climbing the walls for relief.

Besides my hormones taking over, making me want him every moment of the day, my insecurities were creeping back in. I knew it was due to him trying to get hold of himself, but I couldn't help the loss I felt.

That was how I ended up sitting at the table with my hands wringing in my lap while he heated up the dinner Sarah brought over. I closed my eyes, took a deep breath to center myself and spoke the corny words Dr. Morgenson told us about. "I…I need lovey hugs."

Nathan turned and cocked his head, giving me a curious look. I supposed he was wondering why I was using such a silly phrase. He began to smirk, and I could tell he was going to tease me before recognition dawned. His eyes widened, and in a flash I was out of the chair and in his arms.

I sighed and relaxed against him. "I miss you," I whispered into his chest, doing as Darren instructed and telling him why I needed affection from him right at that moment.

Nathan's arms tightened around me as he kissed the top of my head. "I'm sorry, Honeybear, I was trying to cool down. I promised you we wouldn't be intimate like that until I let go."

"I wouldn't label that as intimate."

"No, but it was about to be," he said and nuzzled my neck. His tongue peeked out, licking at my neck. "I want you so bad, baby."

I shivered at his declaration and reveled in the comfort I felt, cocooned in his strong arms. I wasn't sure how long we stayed wrapped in each other's lovey hugs, but we had to reheat dinner.

A few days later when Nathan went off to make dinner, I was free to take a shower by myself. Showers were difficult for both of us in the last few weeks, though Nathan's arousal was much more noticeable than my own. It was torture to watch his cock salute me, innocent brushes against my skin leaving a trail of fire that settled between my thighs. He begged me not to mind, but all I wanted to do was lean forward and take him into my mouth.

I was so happy, getting ever closer to being rid of my cast. I was tired of donning the blue rubber boot to shower and not being able to walk on it.

Once I was ready I stepped into the shower, with the help of the dozen or so handles Nathan added, and sat on the tile seat. The water felt good against my skin, and my body relaxed as I washed the grime of the day away. My hands ran over my body spreading the water around as I rinsed the suds away. I grabbed my razor and, well, trimmed the hedges. Something I'd felt weird about doing in front of Nathan.

Once complete, I moved on to washing my hair. I was rinsing the conditioner from the strands when my fingers brushed over my nipples, and tingles zinged through my body. Thoughts of Nathan in the shower, his cock at full attention, filled my mind. My hand slid down and teased my clit, my fingers sliding against my newly shaved slit.

"Taste me," he begged.

I could imagine wrapping my lips around his head, his fingers tangling in my hair.

"Feels so fucking good. I've missed my little cock slut. So good at sucking me off."

His hips thrust forward, pushing his hard cock down my throat. I imagined my fingers I were his and began pushing them into my pussy.

"So fucking tight. Going to feel so fucking good wrapped around my cock. You'd like me to fuck this tight little pussy, wouldn't you?"

"Yes, please!" I cried out to my vision.

"Do you want my cock, baby? Tell me, tell me how much you want my cock in that tight snatch."

My fingers were pumping faster and faster. "Please, oh, I need your cock, Nathan. Please, fuck me!"

"That's my good girl. God, baby, I need you."

"Take me. Take me so hard I can't fucking breathe."

I moved four fingers into my pussy and began pumping at

a furious pace; all while imagining it was Nathan. My body was tensing as I approached the ledge.

"Come for me, baby. I want to watch you fall apart."

I did as my fantasy requested. I let go, my body shaking as I came for the first time in weeks. Wave after wave of pleasure crashed over me. It was one of the most intense orgasms I'd ever experienced.

Stepping out of the shower, I felt relaxed and refreshed. I toweled off my body and hair, and then wrapped the towel around my torso. I hobbled through the door, but didn't get far when I was assaulted by one of the most sensual and sexy sounds I'd ever heard.

I turned to find Nathan standing next to the bathroom door, his hand wrapped around his hard, weeping cock, pumping with all his might. His eyes were dark, heavy, and clouded; his breath was coming out in pants between his curses.

It was at that moment I realized he'd heard me, my voice echoing off the tile bathroom walls. He'd been listening to me through the door.

I stood there, watching him, and found myself right back where I was before my shower. I should have known it would do no good. He was a sexual creature and my body was always drawn to his.

I noticed that his left hand gripped the door frame so hard he was leaving indentations. Probably to keep himself from doing something he thought we would both regret.

Wanting to help him out, I opened up my towel, exposing my naked body. The reaction I received had me panting for him. His movements sped up; groans and moans slipped passed his lips along with the dirty words I loved to hear.

"Touching yourself in the shower, my horny, dirty girl?

Making me so hard I can't think straight!" he hissed, his hand furiously pumping his cock. "I want to shove my dick so deep, baby. My little fucking cock tease." He licked his lips and took a deep breath, then steadied himself with his hand on the doorjamb. "You're dirtier than anything that can be washed off, that's how much of a filthy little slut you are for me. Only for me. Need another shower? Huh? Too bad. You're not getting one, not after what you just did to me. You're going to watch me and drip. That's what my girl gets. That's what I'm going to give you—a throb, an ache so deep it never goes away."

His jaw was tight, and his face wild with lust, his body almost shaking as his urges took over.

Heat moved through me, my face hot, lips parted as my breathing became more labored. My nipples tightened from the air and from his eyes as they greedily devoured me. It was intoxicating to watch his fist move up and down his shaft, twirling a bit at the head. My pussy ached with how much it wanted him.

He threw his head back, curses streaming from his lips, as hot streams erupted from the head of his cock and landed on his shirt. His body relaxed against the wall, breath coming out in heavy pants. I'd never watched a man do that, and it was so sexy I couldn't take my eyes off him or the moisture seeping into his shirt.

My heart raced in time with my throbbing pussy. Fuck, he was going to kill me. I'd have a heart attack soon if he didn't take me.

He dropped his head and gave me a look of relief mixed with his cockiness since I was gaping at him, and then he moved to the bathroom to clean up while I headed toward the bed. I sat down on the edge and fanned my face in an effort to cool down, but it didn't help as my whole body was in flames.

I lay down on the bed and shut my eyes in an attempt to concentrate on something other than the imagery of Nathan coming, but it wasn't working.

I heard a groan come from somewhere near the bathroom, then a click sound before I felt the soft breeze of the fan.

"Dinner's almost done," he said in a gravelly voice before his footsteps retreated.

The fan helped. His fuck-hot voice did not.

I T WAS A SESSION OF EPIC PROPORTIONS. ONE SENTENCE I THOUGHT seemed so innocent blew up.

"I understand it's in his nature to be dominating and in control, but I can't let someone else control me and what I do."

I had no problem when Nathan wanted to control in the bedroom. It was outside that I had a problem. I'd been controlled growing up; I wasn't going to stand for it as an adult.

Nathan became very defensive when his control issues were brought up. He didn't think he was doing anything wrong, but he couldn't differentiate it in his head.

I mentioned Andrew when he asked for an example. That also did not go over well.

"Andrew is just a friend, he knows me, understands me, and I trust him. He's helped me a lot."

"Oh, here we go." He rolled his eyes. "The always perfect, shining Andrew on the pedestal comes to play. You need more female friends and fewer dicks chasing you around like a fucking tool."

"You have a problem with my past, but I have to deal with

yours? I thought you were friends with him now. You *know* he's just my friend. You have no right to tell me who I can and can't be friends with." My arms crossed over my chest.

"So, you're saying because I don't like you spending so much time with Andrew, I'm controlling?" he asked, twisting my words, his lawyer showing through.

I was having a difficult time sitting still, my spine so rigid it felt like it was about to snap. My legs were coiled tight, either to kick the shit out of him or run away from the conversation—I couldn't tell which one was the stronger reaction. "You told him to keep his fucking hands to himself when all he was doing was helping me out of the wheelchair!"

"Yes, *and*? That's my job. And did you see his face…he was fucking enjoying touching you," Nathan said between clenched teeth. "Is it wrong I hate seeing another man touching you? Is it wrong for me to want to protect what's mine? I love you, and I don't want to lose you. What do I have to do to make you understand?"

I felt like he'd shoved a knife in my chest, the pain of his words cutting me so deeply. My body slumped back against the couch and my gaze moved down to my hands that were twisting in my skirt as I fought the tears in my eyes.

"That's good, Nathan. You told her how you felt instead of shutting her out like you tend to do," Darren said with approval. "He's putting himself out there, Lila, but in turn he's also trying to push you away. Because he's afraid if the Marconi doesn't take you away, Andrew will. He's dealing with some serious insecurity issues here."

"I don't think she'll leave me, I *know* she will." Nathan was fumbling for his cigarettes. He pulled out the pack and fished one out. "I need some air." Nathan left with a huff out the door.

I sat there blinking at Darren, unsure of what to do. Did I go after him, or let him stew?

"Sounds like we hit some nerves." Darren turned to me with a reassuring smile. "This is good, though. You can't put a puzzle back together without all the pieces."

We ended the session there since it was clear Nathan wasn't in a listening place.

Darren hated to send us home in that state, but if Nathan wouldn't cooperate, there wasn't much we could do. He reminded us of our need to communicate before we headed out the door.

We didn't talk on the way home, mostly because we were both still heated from our session and thinking things over. When we reached my condo, I headed to the shower while Nathan went to make dinner. I couldn't wait for my cast to be off so I could go back to morning showers. My hair was always still wet when I woke up, but it took too much time, thanks to my limited mobility, to do it in the morning.

"Can I help?" I asked as I hobbled into the kitchen, fresh out of the shower, a few minutes later.

"Yes, you can make yourself comfortable in that seat right there," he said, directing me to the table.

I rolled my eyes and shook my head. "I want to help make dinner."

"I have it covered. Please just sit down." His voice was tight, the tension quite thick.

He turned back to the spaghetti, while I set one crutch against the wall and hobbled toward the fridge where I knew a bottle of wine was sure to still be hiding. Spotting it in the back, I pulled it out and placed it on the counter. I felt his eyes on me as I located the corkscrew and opened the bottle. I then moved over a few feet and pulled down a wine glass from the cabinet.

He closed the gap between us, stopping right in front of me. "What the hell to you think you're doing?"

"I'm having a glass of wine—what's it look like?"

"No."

"No?"

"No. You're still on some meds and you can't have it." He took the glass from my hand.

"Who the fuck are you to tell me what to do? I want a glass of wine after the day I've had, and I'm going to fucking well have it!"

He hit his boiling point; his arm swung back and threw the glass against the wall. It shattered into tiny pieces before falling all over the tile floor.

I quirked my brow, my eyes locked on his. I stretched out my arm, grabbed the bottle, tipped it back, and took a large sip. Nathan stepped back and dug his fingers into his neck in agitation as he paced in front of me.

I took another sip.

Mmm, good wine.

I stared back in defiance when he stopped in front of me, taking another sip. I set the bottle down and reached up again for another glass.

Before my hand reached the stem, Nathan's hands were on my waist. In seconds I was seated on the counter. Once my disorientation cleared, my hand reached up and slapped him across the face. Our eyes locked and my body was buzzing, electricity radiating off him. It felt like I was coming alive in our fight.

Without warning his lips were on mine, hard and so delicious, but I knew it wasn't what either of us needed. I pushed back against his chest, creating space between us. He stared back at me, and we continued our battle for control. My hand connected with his cheek again.

"Again," he said when he brought his face back to me. I did. "More."

My hands switched and my chest tightened as I repeated, then I lowered my hands and began pounding on his chest. His hands grabbed my wrists, halting my movements as tears slid down my cheek.

He pulled me close to where his chest was flush with mine. "I'm sorry, baby." He pressed his lips to my neck. "So sorry."

My hands fisted into his shirt. "I'm sorry."

"I love you, Lila," he said, his lips trailing up my neck to my lips.

"I love you, too," I replied against his mouth, saying it to him for the first time since I'd said it while doped up in the hospital.

He froze, his lips still attached to mine. He pulled back, the look on his face intense, grave as he realized the magnitude of my declaration. His eyes darkened and then he kissed me again.

His hands roamed under my shirt, setting my skin on fire, grabbing me, pulling my body closer. My fingers tangled into his hair, body arching into his, loving the feeling of him mashed against me.

My head was clouded, lost in my lust for him. I never wanted him to stop, never wanted to have his hands leave my skin, his lips abandon mine.

A fizzing sound filled my ears, and I turned to find the pot of pasta spilling over onto the burners.

"Shit!" He released me and rushed over to remove the pot from the heat.

The distraction brought us back, clearing our heads. He helped me down from the counter, and I moved to sit at the table as he finished preparing dinner.

We were getting so close to having what we wanted. I could see the proverbial light at the end of our twisted tunnel.

I sat out on the patio of Nathan's condo, enjoying the sun and the scenery. He really did have a spectacular view of the city, much better than mine. Erin picked me up from work and wanted to show me the progress that was made on Nathan's… remodeling.

I was shocked when I clamored in to find one half of the entry with smooth, white walls and the other showing the studs. I was told a little more about the destruction he caused, but I was *not* prepared to see the results. The pain he was in was almost palpable weeks later; it was evident in the few sparse pieces of drywall that remained.

Erin had been none too pleased when she showed me the mess he had created in the living room about a week prior. The destruction I witnessed was the evidence of Andrew's offer to stay with me that night. The only night Nathan wasn't with me since the accident.

"Penny for your thoughts?" Erin asked as she handed me a glass of lemonade and sat in the lounge chair next to me.

I sighed. "Just, thinking about Nathan and me."

"I think things are going well."

"You do, huh?" I asked with a small smile before I took a sip of the sweet, tart drink.

"Yes. Nate was brighter this past week. I don't know what

happened between you two, but the air seems…clearer around you both."

"Clearer?"

"You know what I mean." She waved her hand in the air. "There's been so much pain and hurt, it made a constant tension, a static, since your accident. Now, though, I don't know how to describe it. It feels…lighter."

"Yeah, I know what you mean. And, to an extent, things are lighter. We're both trying, but it's rough. I've never felt so much for someone, it's disorienting."

Erin shrugged her shoulders. "That's love."

Two words, one simple sentence, equaled a truth that rocked me. I was not only in love with Nathan, but Nathan loved me in return.

It was hard to believe six weeks had passed since my accident. So much had changed between us in that time. I still didn't know what to call us or our relationship. It was all a bit confusing, but only if I thought about it. Doing it, being in it, loving him, was simple and easy. It was all the baggage we both came with that caused the greatest hurdle. We were both struggling, with Dr. Morgenson's help, to get better, and we were making progressive strides through the muck.

We became pretty self-sufficient again with my limited but gained mobility. He was still staying in my condo, his all but abandoned, and sleeping in the same bed. We stopped putting up the invisible barrier in the bed and often fell asleep holding hands or touching in some way. We also woke up snuggled in each other's arm. I was beginning to feel so much warmth and security there, it scared me, but I tried to push the fear away.

Sarah, Teresa, Erin, and Caroline still helped out on occasion, especially with doctor's appointments and taking me home from work.

Caroline was reluctant to welcome Nathan back in the fold. She didn't trust him with me but was giving him the benefit of the doubt for my sake. She was watching him like a hawk though.

There were occasional dinners that popped up in my condo from time to time. One time there were three dinners that showed up. Needless to say, we were eating well. It was a good thing since I'd lost almost ten pounds through everything, and all the food was helping me to put it back on.

I spent my first three weeks back to work as part-time. Owen was doing a great job. He was a fast learner and a great help to Nathan and me. Hopefully they'd keep him in the position, for a little while at least.

When Jack Holloway called both of us into his office on my last part time day, I thought it was to discuss how things were going and to find out what Owen would be doing. Now donned with crutches, I hobbled through the door Nathan held open and we both made our way to the plush leather chairs sitting in front of Jack's desk.

"Well, it's been three weeks since you returned, Delilah, how are you feeling these days?" he asked.

I stowed the crutches beside me. "Better, and even more so when I get this cast removed."

"Good. Very good. I remember when Nathan was the same," he said with a nod. "How are you two doing?"

My brow scrunched at his question. "Well, we still have mountains of cases on our desks."

"I don't think that's what he's asking," Nathan said. I turned to find him staring at Jack, an inquisitive look on his face. Jack smiled back. "Jack?" There was a pause as they looked at one another. Nathan rubbed his face and groaned. "He knows."

"Knows?" I asked before realization dawned. I turned to look at Jack who was…smiling. Not the image I had in my mind when I thought of our boss finding out about us.

I had visions of a red-faced Mr. Holloway screaming about company policies and how could I corrupt his son-in-law or something. Though I'm pretty sure Nathan was the one doing the corrupting.

"And here I've been freaking out on how to tell you, and you knew!" Nathan threw his arms into the air. Jack smiled bigger and Nathan cocked his head and stared at him. "Jack, why are you smiling? Wait, yo-you didn't…plan this…did you?"

I turned toward Jack and stared in shock. Was Nathan correct?

Jack continued to smile, a smug expression on his face. "Before you came here, Nathan, neither one of you was living. You both went through the motions, both dead on the inside. I hoped that you would be able to help one another."

Nathan shook his head, his brow scrunched, disbelief in his voice as he spoke. "You were playing matchmaker?"

I was too stunned to even say anything. He brought us together. The initiator of the non-fraternization policy in our company.

"Nate, I love you as if you were my son by blood; you will always be my son. I couldn't stand to see you like that anymore. Watching you push us all away. You were never going to heal that way."

"But, Sadie and Will… You were going to fire one or both of them," I said, still slow on the uptake.

Jack sighed. "I really hated to see Sadie go. We were already thinking about altering the policy when we found out. By then it was too late. The good thing is they already decided she was going to stay home with the baby. I wrote a letter of recommendation for her to use in the future."

My head was spinning. Jack planned it? Put us together on purpose? "Why me? How did you know I was…dead inside?"

An apologetic look flashed on his face; he felt guilty. "It was little things I noticed about you, and one was that you wore the same expression Nathan did when you thought no one was looking. Also, when I received your background check…I was quite disturbed by what I read. Filed for emancipation at sixteen. I needed to know more, so I looked into it."

I tensed, and my eyes widened. He knew. Mr. Holloway knew.

"Yes, Delilah, I know about the abuse you suffered at the hands of your family. You were broken. I studied you in the office for weeks. It was the little things. You kept to yourself, besides Caroline. You avoided eye contact and shied away from men who bared any resemblance to your father or stepbrother."

I froze, staring at him in horror. "But, why? Why would you look me up? Dig into my past?"

Jack's head bowed. "I apologize. I know it was wrong."

"I don't get why?"

"I'm sorry. I never intended for you to know I had gone so low, that I ever doubted your loyalty to the company."

My loyalty to the company? My chest tightened, and I found it difficult to force out the words. "When did you…"

"Four years ago."

I heard a gasp to my right and looked at Nathan. Four years ago, Jack lost his daughter; Nathan's wife.

"Why then?" I asked.

"Antonio," Jack said, and I stared at him confused. "When the relationship with Antonio and Karen blew up, shortly after… It was maddening, what I found out, and I became obsessed. I had to know everything about *all* of my employees. I was not going to allow anyone else to get hurt. Any background check that came back questionable, I dug into. Yours was the one of greatest concern to me at that time, Delilah."

"Why me? What happened that would make you do all that?"

"Antonio was using Karen to gather information for him. It was when Antonio was caught with another woman that Karen went off and spilled everything. None of us knew… I trusted Antonio."

"You aren't making sense. What is the deal with Antonio?" Nathan was just as confused as I was.

I was there when things blew up, but it was becoming apparent I didn't know anything about the sordid details. "You put the non-fraternization policy up because of them. I don't see the connection."

Jack swallowed hard and looked straight at Nathan. "Antonio has a cousin he's very close with. I didn't know. No one but Karen did. Antonio is Vincent Marconi's cousin."

Nathan's eyes widened and his hands began to shake, evidence of the panic boiling inside him. I slipped my hand into his, and he squeezed it. He brought my hand up to his lips, placing a light kiss there and he took a calming breath.

"They killed my daughter. It made me sick to know someone close to me fed them information to end the lives of my family," Jack said. His composure faltered, tears brimming in his eyes. "Excuse me."

"The rumors said Antonio was fired because he attacked Karen." I wondered now what the truth was.

"He did. He became angry when she said she was ending their relationship, and she wasn't going to help him any longer. She said she was going to go to the police and expose him," Jack explained. "Antonio didn't take to kindly to that. We found him with his hands around her neck, Karen pinned to the floor. I'm thankful we made it in time. It was a combination of that and the lawsuit by her that followed. Those were the reasons we put the policy in place—to protect our employees and the company."

"What happened to Antonio?" Nathan asked.

"Antonio was put in jail for assault and battery. Karen pressed charges, and I've been working with the Feds ever since to make sure he stays in jail for a very long time."

"What about Karen?" I asked, afraid I already knew the answer.

Jack's eyes saddened, his voice dropping. "Karen disappeared before she could testify." Nathan tensed beside me. "She's probably fine. More than likely, the Feds put her in witness protection. Don't worry."

Nathan was going to have a full-blown panic attack if he kept on the current train of thought that was circling in his head. I knew it would lead him to me and thinking about if they made me disappear. He would pull away, and I wasn't going to allow that again. I was going to be with Nathan, Marconi be damned.

"When did you put this massive plan into motion?" I turned to Jack, trying to draw the conversation away from Karen's disappearance.

Jack smiled at that, still happy with his plan and the outcome. "When I decided to move you and Vivian into the same space, I did so with purpose, more so than simply you two sharing duties. I had already contacted Nate and offered him the position."

"But, that was four months before Vivian left," I said in shock. He'd planned it, planned the whole thing.

That caught Nathan's attention, and he was back in the conversation.

"I had to give Nathan time to take a few classes and get caught back up after being away for a few years, before I fired Vivian."

Nathan snorted and shook his head. "The combined office was a set up."

"Yes," Jack revealed. "I really hoped you two could help one another. I want you both to be happy. She wouldn't want this for you. She would want you to move on, not trapped in this purgatory you've created."

"How do you know what *she* would have wanted?" Nathan asked with a scowl on his face.

Jack's expression faded. "Because that was her nature. She always wanted you to be happy."

"It's so hard," Nathan said. The pain was evident in his voice.

"Why?" Jack asked.

"Why is she dead, Jack? Why is your daughter buried six feet under?"

Jack sighed. "Because there are bad people in the world, Nate. You can't control what they do. No one can, so we deal with it and move on."

Jack's reveal still had me in shock days later. Not only did he know about Nathan and me, he orchestrated the entire thing. He said it was still going to be a few weeks before the new policy rolled out, and even then, Nathan and I were not safe. It allowed two people to be in a relationship as long as they were not in the same section, such as Nathan and me, or directly over someone.

So, we would remain in hiding until we figured out what to do professionally. Overall, we thought it best to stay as is—secretive about our relationship. We didn't need any added stress at the time.

Nathan was acting strange. He had an overwhelming desire for me to see the remodeling of his condo. I reminded him I'd seen it a few weeks prior with Erin, so I didn't know what he was going on about, but followed anyway.

He held the door open and I hobbled through, where he picked me up and headed toward the darkened living room. He set me down and I turned in his arms, only to be blinded by the light coming on and a loud "Surprise!"

Standing in Nathan's condo were all my friends and my family smiling and awaiting my response: Teresa and Armando, Caroline and Ian, George and Sarah, Erin and Trent along with their little boys, and Andrew. I was stunned speechless, as well as confused until I looked to see a huge banner hanging above the mantle that said "Happy 30th birthday, Lila! We love you!"

It was my birthday? I hadn't even noticed, like every one that came before.

I looked around the room and found a beautiful cake decorated in varying shades of red from wine to pink, a table full of gifts, and one full of food and drinks. There were even party hats which I had no doubt were Erin's doing. Best of all, the walls were sans holes.

I was so overwhelmed; my lower lip began trembling, my eyes stung with tears, and I turned into Nathan's chest. My fingers clenched around the fabric of his shirt, and he wrapped his arms around me and pulled me tight, placing a kiss on the top of my head.

"Happy birthday, Honeybear," he said.

The tears left my eyes, slipping down my cheeks.

Everyone came over, and Nathan released me so I could give them all hugs. They all wished me Happy Birthday, told me they loved me, and were happy I was better.

We all had a wonderful evening, my first birthday party… ever. We ate, drank, told stories, laughed, drank some more, opened presents, and enjoyed each other's company. It was the perfect celebration.

I was presented with the beautifully decorated birthday cake, another first, and blew out the candles, making my very first birthday wish. I knew what I asked for was a lot, but I also figured I had twenty-nine previous years of wishes I was due.

Nathan woke with a start, jostling the bed. I was blinded when he turned on the light, and he began a frantic search in the nightstand.

"Nathan?" He jumped from the bed with the dream journal Dr. Morgenson had given to us in his hand.

"I'll be back soon," he said, walking out into the living room. I lay back down and tried to get to sleep, but I tossed and turned with worry.

Sniffles echoed off the walls, cutting through the silence of my condo. He was crying.

I must have fallen asleep not long after because an hour later, Nathan was shaking me awake. I shifted to face him. The expression he wore confused me; it was triumphant yet filled with sadness. In his hand was the journal.

"I need you to read this," he said, motioning to the book in his hand. "I need you to know."

My eyes blurred, and I tried to focus to grab hold of it, but couldn't. It was only four in the morning, after all.

"Will you read it to me?" I asked.

He nodded and slid onto the bed next to me, and I curled into his side as he began to read.

The world always seems to stay the same, but a person grows and evolves constantly. From infant, to adult, and beyond. When you are younger, you're invincible, but it only takes one act to realize you are far from it and one act can destroy you.

I was dreaming. God and the Devil were playing a game of Chess, and I was the pieces. Each time a piece was taken, it was destroyed, turned to dust. Like in Wizard Chess in Harry Potter.

A dark version of me, cloaked in shadow, was me at the point between the time in which I lost Grace and met Lila; he was played by the Devil. A light version that reminded me of myself fresh out of college, full of life, was being played by God.

In my sleepiness I confirmed that Nathan had much more interesting dreams than I did.

I noticed the hand of the King on the light side had a red string wrapped around his pinkie finger, the end dangling down, and the dark version had a pile of ash in his hand.

It was an odd dream to have; I'm not religious. It was even odder when I realized all the pieces were protecting not the King, but the Queen. The dark me had the morbid decaying Grace, while the light me had a broken winged angel Lila.

My mind woke more at his last sentence. Me, an angel? I was nowhere near angelic, broken wing or not.

If I really thought hard, it wasn't that odd.

I watched as they strategically played the pieces. Pawns were lost, bishops and rooks broken to bits, and castles crumbled to the ground until all that was left in the middle of the board were the two Kings. The Queens stayed locked in place. The rules were different, but I supposed God and the Devil could make up whatever rules they wanted.

The ultimate showdown began, and I watched my two halves fight for survival.

There was a loud, splintering crash, and when the dust settled, the victor was revealed.

I was awake, my mind immersed in his story. My body tensed as Nathan paused. We had reached the climax. I knew, just knew, the outcome would define our future.

The light.

I stopped breathing, my body frozen, curled up against his. Was it true?

God won and beat the Devil. He laughed jovially while the Devil cursed.

The light King ran across the board to Grace and took her to God, begging him to let her in and keep her safe. God agreed, saying her soul was already safe and she was happy in Heaven. He said he had a message from her.

"Be safe," God spoke in Grace's voice. "Be happy. Live, Nathan. Live for the both of us, make the most of it. Love with everything you have, and don't be afraid. Fear is a product of the Devil. Don't let him rule you."

He made her a promise of affirmation before rushing over to the broken angel, taking her into his arms and declaring his love and life to her. She too, had a red string hanging down from her finger, and when she took his hand the two strings came together, binding them as one before disappearing in a flash of brilliant light.

Tears pricked my eyes when he spoke of the red string.

The red string of fate: soul mates. Destined lovers regardless of time, place, or circumstance.

When I awoke, I reflected on the dream and realized why it was that Lila was the angel. My time with Grace was up; her thread of life was gone. Lila was hope. She was love, and she was life. She would be my resurrection, and in this new life, the fates would bind me to her and she would make me whole.

I lay frozen in his arms, taking in his dream, lost in thought.

Could it really be this was Nathan's mind saying enough? That he had overcome his final hurdle needed to be over Grace? He had reached acceptance after all this time?

My head moved up to look at him, hoping what I understood his dream to mean was indeed the truth.

"I will always love Grace, and I will always hurt when I think about her and my son, but they're gone now. You are my everything, my future, my Lila. I'm *in* love with you. I'm so in love with you I can't even imagine my life without you. You fill my heart and make me whole. No one will ever compare to you or the way you make me feel. If she met me now, I doubt either one of us would want the other. She couldn't handle the real me the way you can. With you, I am reborn."

I stared at him in disbelief, uncertain of how to react or what to say.

There was only one thing I knew for certain: birthday wishes really do come true. My mind was spinning with the dream he had read to me.

"I don't need you to say anything," he started, his eyes gazing into mine. "I needed you to hear me out. I'm ready to let go of some of the guilt that holds me back."

Holy. Shit. I wanted to pinch myself to make sure I was awake. Was it for real, or was it simply a dream?

My emotions were all over the place. Was this an impulse? Would he retreat back into himself in the morning?

I really didn't want to get my hopes up, but his past behavior left me guarded.

"Take your time. I want you to think about what I said. We'll talk more in the morning," he said, kissing my forehead and snuggling back under the covers, lingering longer than normal. He pressed a few more light kisses at my temples as he pulled me close.

My forehead tingled as it always did when he kissed me there. Sweet and simple, a contrast from his kisses in the beginning of our relationship, but it held so much more meaning than the demanding ones. I liked the demanding ones as well, a lot.

No matter how hard I tried, I couldn't sleep. My mind

replayed his dream over and over again until I eventually drifted off.

I still hadn't figured out anything the next morning. I wanted to believe it with every fiber of my being, but the sting of the past kept rearing its ugly head.

We got dressed and the air was different. Very tense, but also uplifting.

"I want to talk to Darren about your dream." He nodded in understanding. "I just...I..."

Nathan stepped toward me and leaned forward, placing a kiss on my forehead. "I'll give him a call and set up an appointment today."

I sighed with relief. I didn't need to say it; he knew because he felt the same way. We needed Dr. Morgenson's help for something that big and momentous.

As soon as we entered the office, he was on the phone, making an appointment. The effort did not go unnoticed. He wanted it, needed it, as much as I did.

A short while later a text message popped up on my cell phone.

Couldn't make appointment for today, so meeting him for dinner at Erin and Trent's. Will talk then.

Dinner couldn't come soon enough.

IT WAS ALMOST SEVEN WHEN WE PULLED UP TO TRENT AND ERIN'S home, a large two story in a nice suburban neighborhood. The walk up to the door was tense because we both knew Nathan's dream held so much significance and were in desperate need of Darren's guidance. It seemed like we couldn't do anything without his input anymore; we didn't want to screw things up again.

Erin answered the door, her bright smile slipping as she took in our appearance. I was sure we looked as off as we felt. "Hope you two are hungry."

Neither of us said anything, but our fingers were intertwined as we stepped through the doorway.

Trent came down the stairs, his gaze moving from us to Erin, who shrugged her shoulders.

"Good to see you guys." Trent stepped forward to give us a hug.

We moved to the dining room to find Darren sitting with Alec and Brennan, going over Alec's latest drawings. Trent's parents were on their way over to take the kids to dinner so there would be no interruptions.

Darren studied us, most likely trying to understand our behavior and need to see him, but he stayed with small talk for the moment. Erin and Trent looked at each other a couple times, but didn't say anything. It didn't seem strange to us, but maybe that was because we were in it together and knew what was going on.

We sat at the table and Erin passed out margaritas, which I began devouring. I was going to need it to get through the night. Nathan glared at the drink in my hand but didn't say anything. I could tell he was mentally going through what medications I was still on. After a few minutes, he must have been satisfied the yumminess in my hand wouldn't interact much with any of them, and the scowl left his handsome face.

He picked up the glass to join in, and I pulled it from his grip. He turned to me, surprised. "You're on pain meds, and you're driving."

He gave a heavy sigh and nodded, while I moved the glass to my side of the table, happy to have the refill I was going to need.

Nathan had good days and bad days in regard to the amount of pain he was in, but the last few weeks the bad outweighed the good. Taking care of me and carrying me around, had taken its toll on his glued together body. The stress of it all had him in more pain than normal. Though it had been lessening since I'd become more independent, it still made me feel a little guilty I was the reason he ached.

"So, how are things going?" Erin asked, diving right into it.

Trent groaned, and our faces fell. Darren shook his head before saying, "Erin, I don't think that topic is appropriate dinner table conversation."

"I'm only asking a simple question."

Darren chuckled. "Always the inquisitor."

"What?"

"You know that question isn't going to get a simple answer, and you're being nosey," Nathan said, pointing a chip at his cousin.

Erin pursed her lips, unhappy about not knowing what was going on. "Well, then, what can I talk about? What is a safe topic, Nate?"

I was munching on some of the chips and guacamole Erin made. "Oh, what about Erin's cooking skills? This guacamole is fantastic!"

Trent mouthed a "thank you," while Darren and Nathan chuckled. Erin's face lit up and she went into telling me all about the ingredients she used.

It was a Mexican-themed meal with enchiladas as the main course—Erin's specialty.

After dinner Darren led us into the den, directing us to the couch before closing the door and then sitting in one of the chairs. I pulled Nathan's dream journal from my purse and handed it to Nathan, who in turn handed it to Darren.

We were both anxious as he turned on his doctor mode and spent the following fifteen minutes reading over Nathan's dream, his face void of emotion the entire time. Every once in a while he would look up to Nathan and then turn to me before returning his attention back to the journal.

"Hmm," was all he said, the only noise he uttered as he read the intricate details of Nathan's subconscious.

He set it down and sat back in his chair, staring at the journal. It sat there for a few minutes before he picked it back up and read through it again.

My brow scrunched together. *That's it?*

That was when he turned to me. No, that was not it. "I assume you've read this. How does this make you feel? Do you have doubts about the sincerity? Are you scared? Tell me what's going through your head."

I clasped Nathan's hand in mine and took a deep breath before spilling every thought that was running through my head since the previous evening. "I love Nathan, and I want to believe this is what we've been waiting for, but at the same time I don't know if I can trust it. Do I take it at face value? I mean…can it really be true?"

Dr. Morgenson nodded. "It can, if you allow it."

"How does one dream change a man overnight? He could wake up tomorrow and regret it, or decide I'm not enough. What do I have that holds him? Nothing. Because despite how much I try and how much I've healed, I still don't have very much self-worth. So, why would this one dream make every-thing okay, make him want me, and want to stay with me? I'm afraid of what it could or couldn't mean, and I'm afraid… " I trailed off, my head dropping, tears stinging my eyes.

Nathan squeezed my hand as his other hand tilted my face up to his. "I can't let go of all my guilt, but I'm ready to move forward. I think that's what it means. I need to live again, and I want to do that with you. I can't keep going the way I've been heading, and I can't lose you. Honeybear, after everything that's happened, I know I can't be without you." His thumb began to make small circles on my cheek, wiping away the tear that fell. I leaned into his touch. "I love you, and I want us to move forward and out of this purgatory *we've* created."

I leaned forward and placed my lips on his. He pressed into me, his lips parting.

"I want that too, but you have to remember I'm always going to need constant confirmation you want me."

"Then I'll tell you every single day how much I love and adore you, how much I want you in every single way a man could want a woman."

There was a throat clearing, knocking us out of the little bubble we were hiding in. We both turned to find Dr. Morgenson studying us. He leaned forward and placed the journal back on the table and tapped on it. "This? This has rendered me speechless. I mean...wow. I'm astonished, Nathan. This is the largest breakthrough I've ever seen with you, next to admitting you were in love with Lila. You seem to be doing well on your own. I almost feel like my children are leaving the nest," he said, joking with us a bit before asking the question we wanted the answer to. "So, what's the next step?"

Nathan turned to look at Dr. Morgenson. "We were hoping you would tell us that."

"Well, you two have made quite a lot of progress over the past few months. While you both still have a long journey ahead of you, I believe you both may have passed your greatest hurdles." He sat back, contemplating his next statement. "If you were ready to try a conventional relationship, I would encourage it. You two have only made the progress you have because of one another. The love and support you provide one another is healthy, even if your past relationship was not. I have faith in you two. It won't be easy, but you're moving in the right direction."

Dr. Morgenson left us after that to check on dessert, closing the door to the study behind him. We sat there for a moment going over what he had said in silence.

Out therapist thought we were good for one another, that

we helped each other. He was surprised by Nathan's break-through and believed it to be true.

He's the expert, so I should believe him… right?

I was so lost in my thoughts with my hand lying limp in Nathan's, I almost missed the statement that would solidify my decision to be with him.

"I need lovey hugs."

It was then I realized I was acting distant, that he needed almost as much reassurance as I did. I launched myself as best I could from my position on the couch and onto his lap. My arms wrapped tightly around him, my hands fisting into his shirt.

"I love you, Nate. I love you so much."

"Lila, Lila, baby, you are my everything."

We stayed that way for a few minutes before he helped me stand and walk back out to the dining room. Darren, Trent, and Erin were waiting for us. We ate cheesecake with cherries and caught up on idle gossip for about an hour.

It was nice to be with people in a normal setting, doing normal things, and I didn't want the rest of the evening to seem rushed, but I was dying to get out of there and get home. I wanted nothing more than to be in bed, with Nathan between my thighs, his body surrounding mine.

We were getting ready to leave, hugging goodbye, when Erin whispered in my ear. "Much clearer."

The drive wasn't long, but the air was charged, our fingers entwined. We entered the building and stepped into the elevator that would take us up to my condo. The tension in the small space was palpable. It felt like any second the car would explode, but I had a feeling neither of us would mind. My eyes were locked on the panel, watching it change with each floor. Four, Five, Six, Seven.

Before we hit eight, my crutches were on the ground, and I was wrapped up in Nathan's arms, pulled as close as possible to his tight chest. His lips found mine, and it was electrifying. I could feel his need through his fingers.

I'd missed his lips on mine, the connection we had when we were together. He set me on fire and made me feel alive. What we shared sexually was unique, ours, and I'd missed it all and ached to have it again.

The elevator pinged for our floor as Nathan picked me up. I wrapped my legs around his waist, one of his hands holding up my casted leg, while he picked up my crutches. We stumbled down the hall and somehow managed to unlock the door. He tossed the crutches to the ground and walked us back to the bedroom.

He threw me down on the bed and rid himself of his shirt before bringing his lips down to mine. His fingers worked at my waistband, pulling my skirt down over my hips and down my legs.

A rumble moved through his chest as he growled into my ear, "I need you, baby."

My hand moved down his chest, pushing beneath the waistband of his slacks to find what *I* needed. He hissed when my fingers wrapped around his cock. He was hard and hot, and I was getting wet with every second his silky shaft was in my hand.

Hard, frantic hands ripped my shirt from me, and I was forced to let go of my prize. His mouth closed over my nipple, his teeth biting down and tugging, pulling on the sensitive flesh and sending sweet pleasure down to where his hand was working my clit.

I cried out and shuddered, my body begging for more. Heat

trailed along my thigh where his cock brushed against the sensitive skin. So close, so close to where I needed him. My nails dug into his arms from the intensity of it all.

"That's it, baby. You like that, don't you? Fucking begging for it, because…because…"

His voice dropped as he trailed off, unable to finish his sentence, and his movements slowed, while his eyes grew wide. He dropped his forehead to mine, his lips pressed into a hard line. Fuck, he was warring with himself. He was holding the beast back, keeping his lips sealed. I didn't know why he stopped, but I was going to get him back on track.

"Talk to me, please. Please," I begged, my hands roaming his arms and chest. I kissed along his tense jaw and whispered in his ear, "I need it. Tell me how much you love being inside me. How much you need me. How much you love to fuck me hard. How I'm a dirty little slut for letting you do naughty things to me. All the while you fuck me like the whore I am for you. Only for you. All for you. I want you, Nathan. Now. Hard."

He growled, and my pussy clenched from the delicious sound. His hands were rough as they grabbed mine, pushing them into the bed while his body covered mine. He stared into my eyes, the tip of his cock at my entrance, hips thrust forward, driving him as deep as he could go.

My mouth opened in a silent scream as he filled me for the first time in months. An overwhelming feeling took hold, and I trembled in his arms.

Something clicked then, and everything was right. *We* were right.

"Because you are *my* dirty girl. Your moans are mine, your orgasms are mine, your body is mine," he said through clenched teeth. "You are fucking *mine!*"

"Yes!"

"Only my hands will touch your bare skin. Not Andrew, not the guy downstairs, no one but me."

"Only you. It's only ever been you," I whimpered as his slick cock moved at a furious pace, driving me into madness. "Only ever you."

"I *know* when you're dripping for me. I *know* when your pussy is ready for me. And I *know* what you sound like when you're about to come from my cock being inside you." His teeth nipped at my jaw. "No one else will ever know these things about you—only me."

I'd almost forgotten about my casted leg, until I tried to wrap my legs around his waist. The weight of the plaster caught me off guard, and I whacked Nathan in the thigh. He groaned, but didn't stop. Grabbing my leg under my knee he brought it up, pushing it toward my chest. I felt a bump run down my leg and a "shit, fuck," come from Nathan.

My eyes opened and Nathan crashed his lips to mine, groaning again. His hand slammed my left leg down on the bed, while my right leg was swung over his shoulder. He straddled my casted leg and leaned forward, pushing himself deeper at the new angle.

"Fuck, baby, so fucking tight."

My hands wound up in his hair, pulling him down into a kiss. He grabbed hold of my wrists and tore them from him. Pinning my right arm above my head, his fingers entwined with mine, while my other arm was pinned to the bed by my side.

His breath was hot and heavy by my ear. "Hold on, my little whore, I'm going to tear you up."

I shivered at his words and my body was set alight. I tried to move, but the new position and his tight hold kept me in place.

Then it began.

Hard, relentless, pounding, and I was restrained, unable to do anything except feel all of him. In and, just as fast, out. Over and over, harder and harder, as fast as he could go. I was screaming, crying, begging. Words falling from my lips as I clenched around him in one of the most intense orgasms I'd ever experienced.

His mouth was latched onto my neck, nipping, biting, licking, and scraping.

"That's it, take it, take me. Come all over my cock."

The intense pace continued, not allowing me to come down before building me right back up as I climbed toward another orgasm. My body was shaking, and every time he pushed forward or bit down, the fire grew.

"Nathan… Nate, please. I can't…"

"Take it!" he roared, slamming harder, and I crumbled. "You will take all my cock has to give you!"

Tearless sobs erupted from me as I fell over the edge, again. His movements became erratic and his body tensed. His teeth dug into my shoulder, to the point of pain, as I felt him spill inside me.

His hands went lax before his body collapsed on top of mine. It was a little hard to breathe, but I loved the feeling of him so close as he softened inside me.

As we both struggled to recover, I realized we had come full circle, and the sex was exactly what we both needed; it was how we connected.

"Fuck, my head hurts." His head rose from my neck, kissing his way up until our eyes met.

"I thought sex was supposed to get rid of headaches," I said between pants, my body limp.

"Yeah, but it doesn't help when a cast slams into your head repeatedly…"

My eyes widened as I looked up at him. "So, that's what happened?" I tried to keep the smile from forming on my face, but failed. The imagery was too much, and I began giggling as it played over and over in my mind.

Nathan began to laugh as well and rolled beside me, pulling my leg with him, and I rolled onto his chest.

"I love you, so much," I said, snuggling into him.

I felt a kiss on the top of my head. "I love you too, Honeybear. Cast beatings and all."

As we laid there catching our breath, I couldn't help but note the change. We both knew we had found our way home to each other.

FELT A TWINGE IN MY NECK AND SMILED. I WAS BACK TO WEARING scarves to cover the marks he left, so it was a good thing the cooler weather was moving in.

Every moment we weren't in the office, and sometimes when we were, Nathan had his hands all over my body, and I had mine on his. We couldn't get enough of one another, drunk on the ability to finally touch each other again, and it was bliss.

Every caress brought us closer, every kiss solidifying our connection.

Work was busy, as usual, even with Owen's help, but with the events of the previous days, even the Boob Squad couldn't get me down. I was on cloud nine.

Jennifer, in her usual cleavage-baring garment, cornered me in the middle of the week in the break room as I heated up my lunch.

"You know, Delilah, if you weren't such a frigid bitch I'm sure that someone out there would be willing to warm you up at night. I mean, I know you and Andrew had a thing once, though I have no idea what he saw in you, but I really think a good lay would help you out."

I stared at her. "A good lay?" I burst out laughing, catching her off guard. If only she knew. She stormed out in a huff, not appreciating my laughing at her criticism.

I was giddy all day Friday, bouncing in my chair, high on anticipation. I wondered if this was what I'd always heard about kids on Christmas. Was that how they felt? If it was, I finally understood the analogy.

We'd spent the week in a different, almost euphoric, atmosphere. Nathan and I worked during the day, flirting by text the way we used to, and spent the evening in each other's arms, making up for lost time. Well, lost time and repressed lust. He wasn't holding back anymore, and I was reaping all the benefits.

Nathan wanted our date that weekend to be like any other first date, and not like two people who had been living together for the previous two months. He wanted to pick me up from my condo.

The night before I packed my bag, including my date wear, and had it ready for after work the next day. He wouldn't tell me much, only that we were "getting away from it all." He insisted on it being a surprise.

He showed up at my condo, ringing the doorbell moments after I arrived after work that Friday. He helped me with my bag, down to the lobby, and into the parking lot.

When we sat in the car he turned to me and smirked, kissing my lips before drawing back. In his hand he held a blindfold and had me turn so that he could wrap it around my head.

He was making sure his surprise stayed that way.

My mind wandered through the past days. There had been a sudden change with Nathan and me after we talked to Dr.

Morgenson. The walls had fallen down; the atmosphere around us was full of life and energetic.

It was hope, and I wasn't afraid of it anymore; I embraced it.

Hope was something neither of us had held onto in the past. It made everything we'd been through worth it, because for the first time in my life I felt…complete. I felt wanted, needed. I'd never known the part of me I was missing my whole life was him.

We were communicating. Living life through the hard lessons we'd learned over the previous months. As Dr. Morgenson said, we still had a long road ahead of us, but now we were one. Nathan and I were in it together, walking through life hand in hand.

Whatever came our way, we would handle it together.

We slowed down after what seemed like hours, and Nathan allowed me to remove the blindfold. What I saw when I opened my eyes was far from what I was expecting.

"We're having dinner here?" I asked as we pulled up to what I could only describe as a mansion. The house was huge, and it was sitting on an easy five acres.

The only response I received from Nathan was a grin as we moved up the drive. Once we reached the front door, he hopped out and came around to my side to help me out. He handed me my crutches, and I headed up the stairs to the front door in my usual slow-going pace while he retrieved our bags.

I thought for our first date we would go out to a restaurant or something. Wasn't that what was the tradition? Random mansion outside the city was not what I was expecting.

The door opened before I made it up the last few steps, and I was surprised to see Sarah on the other side.

She smiled at me; her arms open wide in greeting. "Lila! Welcome!"

"Good evening, Sarah." My confusion rose at her being there. Our first date was with his parents?

"Mom, you said you would be gone by four," Nathan said with a groan from behind me. "It's almost six."

"Yes, yes." She waved his words off. "Your father was delayed—you know how it is. Don't worry; we're heading out in a moment so you two will have your privacy."

I reached the top step and she pulled me in for a hug. "How are you feeling today? Are you excited about tonight?"

I pulled back and smiled at her. "Very. Though I'm a bit confused about what we're doing here."

"This was all Nathan's idea," she said. "He wanted to be romantic, but wanted you to be comfortable, so I offered up our house as a little retreat for you two."

"Wow, I'm…impressed." I glanced back at Nathan who was closing the trunk and heading our way.

She held the door wide for me as I hobbled through. "How's your leg doing? You look good, and you're getting around so much better."

I sighed. "I can't wait to have this thing off."

"Just a few more days! Then the two of you can go on weekend trips with ease."

George came down from the second floor moments later and greeted Nathan and me, before the two of them headed out for their own weekend getaway. It would be Nathan and I alone all weekend…not at home.

I wasn't sure what we were having for dinner, but Nathan said we were staying in. We both headed up the stairs to get ready. I began to wonder if we were having deli sandwiches, because there was no one else around to help him cook.

We were in the spare bedroom that would be ours for the

weekend getting dressed when I heard a small laugh behind me.

"Why are you laughing?" I scowled up at him through the reflection in the mirror.

"Because it's sad and ironic at the same time," he said and stepped up behind me, wrapping his arms around my waist.

"What is?"

"I hate it, but you now will have scars that match my own. Together we make one whole person," he paused before continuing, his voice low in my ear. "Together we are one whole heart, one whole soul."

My head craned to look up at him over my shoulder; his eyes were soft, his hand moved to cup my face, his thumb making light circles on my cheek.

My gaze locked on his. "I love you."

His head bent down, and his lips found mine. It was hard and soft, building in intensity until I was somehow turned around and pinned against the wall.

I groaned when he pulled away, the lust in his eyes making me light up. "I need to stop, Honeybear, or we won't make it to dinner."

"We can always stay here." I pulled him back to me.

"Not tonight, baby. You've waited way too long for me to take you on a date."

I pouted when he pulled away, but smiled when he whispered to me, "Later, my little insatiable minx." He nibbled on my ear, and nipped at my neck. "I will make you come again and again."

"Promise?"

"Promise."

He left after that, running downstairs to work on

something, leaving me to finish getting ready on my own. I sat down at the vanity and studied my reflection. I looked as nervous as I felt. My hands were even shaking as I pulled the eye shadow from my makeup bag.

My mind was whirling and not down a good path. It was the first date I'd gone on in years, and it was rather unconventional at that. What if he found out something he didn't like? What if, on our date, I wasn't what he thought I was? What if he found he didn't want me?

Ridiculous, I chided myself. *Not going to happen, Lila. He loves you. He's a good person, and he makes you so happy. This is what you deserve, to be happy with Nathan.*

I squared my shoulders in the mirror and stood up to locate the shoe I would be wearing.

"Lila!" Nathan called out a few minutes later, and I headed toward the stairs.

"Ready!"

He beamed at me and helped me down the stairs; my body buzzed with excitement.

Our first official date.

He sat me down and picked up what looked like my sweater. He began walking, and I followed him through the house, happy to soon be rid of my hindrance. Instead of heading toward the kitchen or dining room, Nathan headed to the back door.

"Where are we going?"

He smiled at me. "Outside."

"Outside?" It was then I understood why he was carrying my sweater.

"Come on, Honeybear," he said, holding the door open so I could get through.

What awaited me on the other side of the door was not what I was expecting. There was a gazebo lit up by strings of lights all around, and candles that sat on an elaborately decorated table.

It was a whole other world nestled in between the trees. Cloth was draped all around, weaving in and out of the intricate wood work. The table was beautifully set and covered in cloth the color of the wine that sat atop it and was sitting next to a bouquet of matching roses.

"Nathan…" I trailed off, so overwrought with emotion.

"Do you like it?" he asked, wrapping his arms around me.

"It's beautiful."

We headed down the lit walkway, tears welling in my eyes. Nathan helped me take a seat, setting my crutches against the wall. He kneeled in front of me, took my head in his hands, his eyes searching mine for discomfort. His body was tense, waiting for my reaction.

I was blown away by it all. "It's so wonderful. I didn't know you had such a romantic streak in you."

After I was done speaking, he relaxed, chuckling as he leaned forward to kiss my lips. "Well, I figured I had a lot to make up for. We should've had our first date long ago." He took a seat and poured the wine. "Plus, my mom helped out with the decorations. She wanted us to feel like we were somewhere else."

There were rolls sitting in a basket we nibbled on. I still wasn't sure what was going on, but received my answer when the back door opened and someone came out with a tray. She placed it on a small table against the gazebo wall and picked up two small plates, setting them down in front of Nathan and me before retreating.

"You hired a waitress?" I looked from the salad in front of me to the retreating form of our silent guest.

"And a cook." Nathan took a bite of his salad. "I wanted to take you out, but it would be difficult for you with your cast still on."

"So you opted for a mix?"

"Exactly."

We worked on our salads, me picking out the tomato and giving it to Nathan, him picking out the olives and putting them on my plate. It was a strange symphony I had a feeling would develop more over time.

"Ah, missed one," he said, picking up the olive with a fork. Instead of placing it on my plate, he held it out in front of my mouth. I let out a small laugh before opening my mouth and letting him put the fork inside. It was going to be an interesting evening.

Dinner arrived, and I cut off a piece of pork and held it on the fork in front of Nathan's mouth. He quirked an eyebrow at me, smiling as he leaned forward to take the bite.

I opened my mouth and pointed my finger toward it while making a little feed me sound. He swallowed hard and his eyes darkened.

"The next time you do that, I will put something in your mouth and you will suck on it, choke on it, and then swallow what I give you."

I drew in a sharp breath and began squirming in my seat. "Promise?"

He growled, stood up, and then leaned across the table. His fingers grabbed hold of my jaw, pulling me toward him. Lips pressed to mine, pouring passion into them, biting my lower lip as he pulled back.

His thumb swept across my bottom lip, then the back of his fingers caressed my cheek. "I'm trying to be good here, baby, but if you keep this up I will pull out my cock right here, onlookers be damned."

"You should know by now that whenever you want me I'm yours."

He took my hand in his and brought it to his lips, placing light kisses. "I know, baby, and don't think I won't take full advantage of it in the future. In public, in private, I'll take you when I want."

I wiggled in excitement for that day to come. He sat back down and stared at me with a heated look.

As we worked on our dinner, conversation flowed, fingers caressed, and happiness surrounded us. It was the lightest I'd ever felt.

I wanted every day to feel like this.

The outdoor heaters kept the chill out of the fall air, along with the wine in our system. Nathan no longer objected to the wine since I wasn't on any medications that could have bad interactions with it.

"Come on," he said, getting up from his chair and walking over to me.

"Where are we going now?" I asked as he scooped me up in his arms.

He smiled at me and kissed my forehead. "Dessert."

"The bedroom?"

He laughed out loud at my comment and shook his head. "No, I have something else planned before I take you there and have my wicked way with you."

Nathan carried me down a small path toward the pool house. The lights were off, a soft glow was created by a candelabra sitting on a small table with a bottle of something and a covered plate. There was a double-wide padded lounge chair covered in blankets that Nathan sat me on before pulling the blankets around me.

He then pulled the cork off what turned out to be champagne. He poured two glasses, handing one to me, then sat down under the covers next to me. It was so romantic, and nothing I could have foreseen happening to me in my life. I sipped the bubbling wine while he pulled the plate and a couple of napkins over. He took the cover off, and I licked my lips in anticipation; there were chocolate covered strawberries filling the dish.

He picked one up, placed it at my lips, and I bit into it, the juice from the berry leaking out and dripping down my chin. Nathan took care of it, his head leaning down, tongue lapping at the trail, following it back up to my lips where he kissed me.

I grabbed one and mimicked him, placing it in front of his mouth. He flicked his tongue at the end and smirked at me before biting into it.

I wanted to be the berry.

I leaned forward and kissed him before he was even done, catching him by surprise. He moaned against my lips and leaned into me, his fingers caressing my neck.

His lips moved against mine, his tongue seeking mine as a strong, slow pace settled over us, and it was different than any other time. His strong hands held the feverishness of his touch, but they were lighter, almost reverent, as they moved along my skin.

"Feel how much I want you, how much I need you. It's all for you, baby, only for you," he whispered, planting kisses along the length of my neck.

It was petting, making out, warming up. Normally we were so worked up that we passed the bases and exploded. He was taking over my body, wrapping me in his warmth, his love.

We stayed under the stars cuddled under the blanket, reveling in each other deep into the night. We were enjoying being together without anything holding us back for the first time.

FINALLY, AFTER SO LONG, MY CAST WAS OFF. MY ANKLE WAS VERY stiff, and I'd lost some muscle, but I could walk on my own, shower without the blue boot, and my freedom returned. I couldn't keep the smile off my face as we left the doctor's office, regardless of how much cave woman leg hair was revealed under that damn thing. Nathan was chuckling at me. He wrapped his arm around my shoulder and pulled me close as we walked to his car.

"If I'd known it would make you this happy I would have ripped that damn thing off of you weeks ago. It got in the way," he whispered in my ear, nipping at my lobe.

"Mmm, yes, but we managed just fine."

He smirked at me. "You didn't get knocked in the head by it multiple times. Really ruins the mood."

I swatted at his arm. "It didn't seem to stop you regardless. And seeing as you had a lobotomy, no harm done."

We stopped in front of the car and he pulled my body flush with his. "Yes, well, I was inside you for the first time in over two months. Do you really think anything, including the ending of the world, could have made me stop?"

I smiled up at him, biting my lip. "Come on, let's go home."

"Excited about something, baby?"

"Yes! A shower without the blue boot!"

He stared down at me, balking. "A shower?" He pouted.

"Yes, but you know very well what can be done in the shower." I winked up at him. "Thanks to all those handles you installed."

His eyes darkened, his fingers clenching. "Shower it is!"

I giggled, yes giggled, at his excitement and got into the car.

Life had taken a definite turn for the better. I was happy for the first time ever.

I had freedom since my cast was removed and was in physical therapy to help gain back strength in my leg. It was incredible to be able to walk on my own and get around, doing everyday simple tasks I took for granted before.

My next step was to drive, and I couldn't wait to do that again.

I'd already planned how it was going to go, but I hadn't told Nathan. I turned to him after work on a Friday before sitting down for dinner. "I'm going car shopping tomorrow."

"Sounds good. Let's eat," he said, pulling my chair out for me.

"Without you."

He held his breath and looked at me in what seemed like slow motion. "Why?" The word was drawn out.

"I want to do this with Andrew. You know I love how possessive you get, but I need to focus on buying a car tomorrow, not worry about how worked up you might get when a slick car salesman gives me a look that has nothing to do with desire and everything to do with making a sale."

"I wouldn't—"

"You would, and you do. Andrew's more reserved and doesn't react like you do. Even if he did, it wouldn't matter, because I don't feel that way about him."

"What way?" He frowned, holding onto his anger, trying to tamp down his natural reaction to go off.

"The way I feel about you. If Andrew gets jealous, oh well. I mean, I don't want him to feel that way about me, but if he did—"

"He does." Nathan's lips twitched.

I couldn't help but roll my eyes. "It doesn't matter. What I'm saying is I can't focus on buying a car; not if you're going to try and claim me during the test drive to prove something that doesn't need to be proved. I've already discussed it with Drew, he's done the research for me, he's knowledgeable about cars, and I trust him."

"I don't." His hands gripped the edge of the table, knuckles white from the force.

"You should. He's done nothing to warrant your distrust." My voice went soft, and I made it as soothing as possible. I reached out and touched the back of his hand. "Please, don't fight me on this. It's not a big deal."

"I want to be a part of these types of things in your life," he said, his eyes pleading with me.

"And you will. But this one I need to be as stress-free as possible." I gave him a sympathetic smile. "Please, trust me."

"I do." He blew out. "I'm trying to trust him."

I opened up his hand, releasing it from the table and leaned my head against his open palm. "Drew and I were a long time ago, and it was nowhere near the depth of us. I tried to open up to him, but he didn't understand."

"He never will, because he's never had to go through something terrible."

I kissed the inside of his hand. "Let's talk to him about this tomorrow. Give him ground rules."

"Give him a cup because he's gonna need it if he gives you any look I don't want."

I shook my head. It was never going to change, no matter what I said. "Men."

"I'm serious—I'll kick him in the nuts so hard he won't be able to sit in any damn car you choose to test drive."

"I'm sure you will." I kissed his cheek, sat down, and he dished up my plate for me so we could finally eat.

Andrew showed up the next morning, smiling and radiating with excitement.

Nathan was the opposite.

"Hey, we need to talk for a minute before we leave to go do this," I said.

He nodded, then gave Nathan a wary look. "What's going on? Did you punch a hole in her bedroom wall?"

"No." I smacked Andrew's arm. "He would never do that to my place."

"I don't do that anymore, anyway," Nathan grumbled.

"Yeah, whatever. I've heard you're still doing that shit and smoking, which I don't like. Lila, don't forget you quit smoking for a reason."

I rolled my eyes. "Will you stop, already? We're not discussing any of that. Quit trying to meddle. Just listen for a minute."

"Fine. What do you need to say that's so important it's keeping us from getting your new car?"

"Sit down, please," I said, motioning to the couch.

Andrew stood rigid in place. "No thanks. I'll stay here."

"Jesus," Nathan gritted, crossing his arms over his chest. "You see… I told you he wasn't going to listen to you."

"I'll listen to anything she has to say as long as it makes sense." Andrew flexed his biceps, which wasn't as impressive—he was so skinny.

"Sit." I pointed at the couch.

Andrew finally did as I asked, heaving an annoyed sigh as he did.

I stood between both of them and took a deep breath. Nathan took a seat across from Andrew, glaring at him.

"I love you, Nathan, and only you," I said before turning to Andrew and speaking to him. "I'm so happy with Nathan. I love our friendship, but that's all it will ever be. I hate seeing the two men most important to me duking it out all the time. This fighting is making me not happy. Do you really want me to be *not* happy?"

They both stared up at me and looked at each other before speaking at the same time. "Okay."

"Keep your hands off her," Nathan said, leaning forward and holding his hand out, offering it to Andrew.

Andrew grinned, taking Nathan's hand. "Hurt her again, Thorne, all bets are off, and I will kick your ass. I may even run over it with her new car if the mood strikes me."

They both laughed and the air seemed clearer.

Men were strange creatures. I didn't get it, but it worked, and I was able to leave without worrying about Nathan being upset.

We spent an entire Saturday visiting car dealerships, trying out all the cars Andrew had formed in his list.

By the end of the day, he had me shelling out way more than I'd anticipated, one and a half times what I'd paid for my Malibu. I called Nathan to get his opinion, and he agreed with Andrew.

The car buying expedition was what brought Nathan and Andrew's friendship back together. Their concern for my safety guiding them to find something they deemed best for me. They were back to having lunch together a couple times a week.

"Tell me why I just spent forty grand on a car?" I asked Nathan as I filed away my loan paperwork the following weekend.

"Because it's a safe car, a good car, a really cool car, and insurance gave you ten grand for your totaled one," he said, wrapping his arms around my waist before continuing. "That and it has tinted windows and a large back seat, making it real easy for me to do very naughty things to you."

I gasped in mock surprise. "You want to defile my new car?"

He shook his head, his lips ghosting across my skin. "No, I want to christen it by fucking you like the good little slut you are, in it. I want those seats dripped wet with your slick come, that's what your car needs, and it's what I need."

I was looking at my car in a whole new light after his words.

Time was flying by with as busy as we were. Work was, as always, hectic. Adding to our couple's therapy, my physical therapy, Nathan's kickboxing, and my art classes and our dates out of town every weekend—there wasn't a moment to breathe!

Busy, but every free moment we had was spent with each other. Always touching, the physical dependence we had on one another was staggering at times.

Every night, we made dinner together, and I was even teaching Nathan how to cook. We became very domesticated, and I had to admit it was…nice. More than nice. It was bonding on a whole new intimate level.

It was hard to be locked together in the office all day and unable to tell him I loved him, or kiss him, or ravage him—one of my favorite things. Just talking was difficult. I couldn't wait for the day when we would be free to express our feelings at any time. In order to do that, one of us would have to leave, and I wasn't ready for that yet.

Jack was close to rolling out the new policy, but we weren't safe, even under the new rules. We both knew time was winding down, but what we didn't know was how long we had to make any decisions.

It was a month after our first official date that a large arrangement of flowers was delivered to my desk. Unfortunately we weren't alone when the delivery was made; Caroline and Tiffany were also in the office.

I pulled the card from the bouquet and opened it up. My heart swelled while I read the words, while listening to Caroline gushing about the bouquet.

My heart is in your hands, keep me safe. I love you.
Christopher

I couldn't help the smile that lit up my face as I read and reread the words written on the card. I'd never been sent flowers, and to have Nathan do it almost brought tears to my eyes. It was

a way for him to communicate without speaking. *Christopher*—
my Nathan.

I scowled, however, when the card was ripped from my hand.
I glared at Nathan, who had Tiffany peering over his shoulder,
as he gazed at the card.

"What mush. You know, most guys who send you flowers
are trying to make you overlook that they're cheating on you. I
bet he's cheating on you," Tiffany said, trying to knock me down
a peg from my flower receiving high.

Nathan tossed the card back over to me. "He sounds like a
pussy to me."

"Oh, shut it, Thorne, you're ruining my moment," I shot
back. My smile returned when I looked over the words again,
warmth spreading through me. Love. I was loved.

He shook his head. "I don't get women and flowers."

"It's sweet. A reminder you're thinking of us when we're
apart," Caroline said as she took a whiff of one of the roses.

"What about the man?"

Caroline turned to Nathan. "Well, enlighten us, what would
a man want?"

Nathan thought for a moment, a smile on his lips.

I rolled my eyes. "You're thinking dirty thoughts, aren't you?"

He grinned wide, and I shook my head as plans sparked in
my head.

It was after six when I deemed the office empty enough for what
I had planned. Getting up from my chair, I moved to the door and
shut it, turning the lock. Nathan's eyes shot to me at the sound,
his eyebrow quirking at my actions.

I stalked over to him, his body turning in his chair to face me, stopping when I was two feet in front of him. I dropped to my knees in front of him, my hands reaching out to his belt buckle.

"Delilah?" he asked, licking his lips and scooting his hips farther down the chair.

I palmed him, moaning at the feeling of him hardening beneath my touch. I leaned forward and nuzzled his cock, my teeth grabbing hold of his zipper and pulling.

"Fuck, baby." His hips rocked up against my mouth as he hissed, his cock hard and ready.

I freed him and licked from base to tip, swirling my tongue around before taking him into my mouth. Humming, I worked my way down, all the way to the base before sliding back up. I could hear him panting above me, whispering profanities; his head tilted back, eyes closed.

"Is this the man's equivalent of flowers?" I asked, sucking him back into my mouth.

"Mmm, getting close, baby."

He grabbed my hands and lifted me off the ground, his cock falling from my lips, and he pulled me to him. My legs opened up as he helped me hike up my skirt so I could straddle his hips. The heat of his erection could be felt through the satin of my panties as I rocked against him, teasing him.

He grabbed the sides of my face and brought my lips to his in a searing kiss. His hands kneaded their way down my waist to my hips, one circling around the front to pull my panties aside. Our kiss broke apart, and I angled up a bit so he could slide right into my aching pussy.

We both cried out as he filled me.

"Too long since you've been wrapped around me."

I lifted my hips and began to ride him. "And you call me the insatiable one."

He chuckled and nipped at my jaw. "Can you blame me? Fucking sexy ass, and then you come on to me by dropping to your knees? Fuck, baby, do you really think I wouldn't want to fuck my little whore?"

I moaned as his dirty talk kicked in.

"Too slow," he said through clenched teeth.

"Can't take it?"

"Fuck no!" he exclaimed and stood, setting me on his desk and brushing piles of papers aside to lay me back. "Hold on."

My two favorite words.

My hands grabbed the desk edge as he quickly slid all the way in.

It was hard, fast, and dirty. Neither of us could deny the excitement that came with having sex in the office, the thrill of the possibility of getting caught.

I would miss it when the end came, but until then I was going to enjoy every second of it.

On Wednesday night he said he had a surprise for me, and I had to be airplane travel ready at the end of the workday on Friday, complete with a swimsuit. He knew I'd never flown before, and the only swimming I had ever done was in the college pool when I took a beginner's swimming class. This left me calling up Caroline and Erin, begging for help to find a swimsuit on short notice at the end of the summer.

The next day I was standing in Caroline's office holding up a tiny scrap of white fabric.

"What is this?" I refused to acknowledge what she said it was.

"It's your bathing suit."

"No, this is a scrap of white cloth barely able to cover my nipples and slit if I'm fucking lucky!"

"Don't raise your voice at me, missy. You needed a bathing suit, I found you one. A hard feat with the season over."

My teeth clenched. "You did this on purpose."

She laughed. "Why the hell would I do that?"

"Because you like to torture me."

She smiled at me, and I glared back. I was right.

Somehow Caroline eventually managed to convince me to wear the tiny white bikini she found on a clearance rack. I about died when I looked at the small scraps of fabric, but I had to admit it looked good on. While I had no problem wearing it for Nathan, he'd seen me in much less very often; it was everyone else we might encounter who concerned me.

We made it to the airport with time to spare, our carry-on suitcases in tow with our personal items.

"You ready?" Nathan asked when they called for our flight. He brought our entwined hands up and kissed my fingers.

My stomach did a flip, then a flop, but I managed to nod and follow him down the passageway to the plane.

It wasn't a long flight, and I freaked out a tiny bit during some turbulence we encountered. By ten in the evening on Friday night, we were checking into a bed and breakfast on the beach in Florida.

"What do you think?" Nathan asked as he opened the windows, letting in the soothing sound of the waves against the shore. A sound machine could never match the real sound of the waves. It was something I found so calming, so freeing.

"Perfect. Nothing but perfect."

It was, and having him next to me meant it would be impossible to ever forget.

AWOKE THE NEXT MORNING TO HOT KISSES AND BREATH ON MY neck, a hand on my breast, fingers in my pussy, and Nathan's cock rocking against the swell of my ass. The second he realized I was awake, I was on my back and he was between my thighs, slipping his cock deep inside me.

Best morning wake-up call ever.

Later that morning I discovered how much Nathan liked the swimsuit Caroline found.

So much he had the ties undone with me sitting on the edge of the dresser, fucking me senseless, within minutes of having put it on.

I'd have to buy Caroline a massage or a nice dinner for her find.

When we made it down to the beach, he couldn't take his eyes off me, and I couldn't even describe the feeling that evoked in me. Though it turned out there were others who also liked the swimsuit.

I tried to brush off the looks I was getting. "They're just staring at my scars."

"Fuck that, they're looking at your sweet little body, baby." He tugged me closer to his side, muttering under his breath.

There were two surfers in particular with ripped abs that kept watching me and smiling whenever I walked along the beach.

Nathan didn't like that very much.

His possessive side took over, his hands never leaving my body. He kissed me, hard and long, more than once to show the male beachgoers who I belonged to.

I rolled my eyes at him. "Why don't you come all over me again? That worked last time."

He smirked, squeezing my ass. "Don't tempt me, baby. I will fuck you on this beach if that's what it takes."

He calmed down a bit when I made sure to switch my attention from the ocean and beach to him. My focus was on him, and I made it obvious I saw only him and no one else. Didn't matter how many dicks were around.

The beach was wonderful. Words couldn't describe how much I loved it. I'd never been, and I loved the feel of the sand beneath my feet, the waves as they chased me up the dune, the push and pull of the tide. However, I did not like the taste of a mouthful of salt water.

Nathan held on to me tight whenever we were in the water, knowing I wasn't a strong swimmer. At one point he pulled me out to a shallower section that met right above my navel.

He wrapped his arms around my waist. "How do you like the beach, baby?"

"I love it. Thank you so much." I stood on my tiptoes to kiss him.

When we released, I couldn't help but let out a little laugh.

"What's so funny?"

I shook my head. "Nothing, it's just…it reminds me of a dream I once had."

"A dream? Of what?"

"The future. Our future. It was when I was in the hospital after the accident, right before I went into surgery. It was on a beach much like this one."

"And what did our future on the beach look like?"

I smiled as I leaned into him. "It was beautiful, so beautiful. Light, carefree, and full of love and children."

Nathan hummed. "I like the sound of all that."

He gave me a warm smile, and the rest of the day continued to be light and carefree.

Our entire stay was like living in that dream I'd had, minus the children.

I didn't want to leave on Sunday afternoon; the trip was heaven. I loved the beach and hoped we could return in the near future for a full vacation. Maybe in that time I could take some more swim classes and become a better swimmer, then I could keep up with Nathan a bit better.

"Baby, everything all right?" Nathan took my hand and moved it up to his lips as we drove to work the following Monday.

"Yeah, I hate that we're back to pretending we loathe each other. It's difficult sometimes, you know? I'm getting tired of it."

"I know, Honeybear, I know. I hate that the best I can do is send you flowers under another name on the card to mislead people. I want everyone to know you're mine—not solely when we're on vacation, but the people we see and talk to every day."

I nodded and ignored the way my chest clenched and almost dropped at the thought of the Boob Squad throwing their tits and innuendos his way again. I hated I was helpless, forced to watch, unable to rip them off him by their hair.

I wanted it to be like he'd been with me at the beach. I wanted to shove it in their faces, make them watch me as I accepted his tongue and other body parts inside me. I wanted them to understand that no matter how many tits were around, he only wanted me and mine.

It was disheartening to know we couldn't do that without risking our jobs.

Fuck. I was missing that Florida beach already more than he'd ever know.

Masks firmly in place, we exited the car and walked in to another busy day.

We decided to stay close to home the weekend after our trip to the beach and drove north to Noblesville. I let Nathan know I wasn't entirely comfortable because of its proximity to where I grew up, but he assured me he would protect me. Chances were low I'd see any of my former family, because they still lived about twenty miles north, but it was also the closest I'd been since I'd left years before.

It was a beautiful fall day, the sun was shining, and it was on the warmer side for the season. Needless to say, the streets were crowded with all the people who were also out enjoying the weather.

We stopped into a little shop that caught my eye. In the window was a large stained glass tree. The stores tag line was: Gifts Inspired by Nature. Inside the store it was full to the brim with fountains, artwork, lawn adornments, clocks, unique soaps, and gifts. This place was different, and I found myself wanting to buy half the items.

What caught my eye, however, hung on the wall just beside the cash register. There was a display of tiles lined six by six, each one varying from the next: paintings of people, figures of animals, letters, music, game pieces, flowing shapes, and abstract works. I didn't know who the artist was, but I was drawn to the distressed look of the tiles and the beautiful artwork portrayed.

I was captivated by two blue birds sitting on a branch, and I wasted no time asking the sales clerk for it. Then I almost died from sticker shock for the one tile, but reminded myself I didn't often find something that struck me as it did.

I wasn't sure what it was about them, but something about the two little birds drew me in. They shared a branch, but weren't looking at one another, if blue birds would even look at one another. Somehow, it reminded me a little of Nathan and me.

As she rang me up, the sales clerk asked me if I wanted to be on their mailing list. I jotted down my information, happy to have a line to a store with such wonderful items, and vowed to return.

Later in the day, the sun was lowering in the sky when we headed out to dinner. Nathan chose a little Italian restaurant, and we had an enjoyable evening.

It was on our way back to the bed and breakfast we were staying at when he decided to make a detour. We weren't far off the main strip when he looked from side to side before pushing me against the brick exterior in a small alley.

His lips were harsh, as bad as the bite of the brick, while his hands grabbed at my flesh, pulling me toward him. I could feel him hard and ready, pushing into me.

His mouth was at my ear, hot and heavy with a smirk in his tone as he whispered to me, "Bad girls bend at the waist."

I nipped at his jaw while my hands pulled him free of his jeans. He backed up a step as I bent down, allowing me access. I sucked him into my mouth, causing him to draw in a sharp breath.

One of his hands tangled into my hair, pushing and pulling me along his length, while the other grabbed at my ass, slapping and groping it.

"Fuck, baby, you're so good at sucking my cock," he moaned, his hips thrust forward, pushing him down my throat, making me choke on him.

He released me, drawing my head up and kissing me hard as he pressed me back against the wall. His eyes flitted around; he was making sure no one was coming before lifting up my skirt. He grabbed one of my legs behind the knee and raised it, opening me up to him. His other hand tore the thin fabric of my panties.

I groaned against his lips. "Not another pair."

He smirked down at me. "I'll take you to Victoria's Secret tomorrow and you can buy all the panties you want."

I felt the head of his cock at my entrance, then he slipped between my soaked pussy lips, stretching me.

"Always so damn tight," he said as he set up a pace. "Do you like this? Being fucked in an alley like a common whore, on display for anyone to see how dirty you are?"

"Fuck, your mouth will be the death of me."

I heard footsteps closing in and began to panic. Nathan's thrusting sped up, becoming faster.

"Not yet, *so* close," he whispered, begging me not to make him stop.

His increased speed was building me up faster and harder until my head fell back against the wall and my mouth opened in a silent scream.

His grip was tight, fingers digging into my ass and leg as his mouth clamped onto my shoulder to stifle his cries while he emptied inside me.

My eyes shifted to the side, the voices and shuffling of feet moving closer until they passed by the alley entrance. Not a single head turned our way, and we remained hidden.

After a moment of rest, he released my leg. We straightened out our clothes and headed back out onto the main thoroughfare. I didn't get very far before I felt it begin to slide down my thigh as we started to walk back, and had to stop in my tracks. Nathan turned to look at me, and I glared at him.

"I hate you."

He had a surprised look that quickly vanished before reaching between my legs under my skirt. His hand moved upward, wiping the trail with his fingers. With his other hand he opened my mouth and placed his come-covered fingers inside. My face flamed as my tongue twirled around his digits, cleaning them.

"You don't hate me, baby. You love how I make you feel. And this is the best taste in the world."

It was true. I did love the way he made me feel, and he was the only one who could make me feel that way.

We continued our walk back, hand in hand, smiling at each other as we enjoyed the end of our beautiful day out.

Things were going great. Nathan and I were happy. We were getting healthier every day.

Inside I knew it would come crashing down on us, just who, what, where, and when were the variables.

Our days were long again, and we were trying to get some ground. Owen was helping us, spending half of his days on our workload and the other half on his own. He was moved to the desk right outside our office, and I smiled every time I heard him recite to one of the Boob Squad members the office dress code. When one would retort that the men didn't seem to be complaining, he would raise his hand. They would then shoot back saying he was gay, and he would come back saying he had standards and skanks were way below his line.

Nathan and I would laugh so hard sometimes we were almost crawling under our desks. Depending on how far the particular member would take it before she found out she was out-smarted, and they weren't going to get a rise out of him in any way.

Needless to say, he was also a great help in keeping the Boob Squad visits down. They would get so irritated by him at times they would forget why they were there and storm off back to their desks.

Owen was a spectacular addition to our team.

He made my missing that Florida beach and my weekend getaways with Nathan that much more bearable.

I turned to Nathan on a particularly harrowing Monday when the Boob Squad was in full force and said, "What would we do without all this entertainment he provides?"

"Fuck on the desk in the middle of the workday and get caught."

"Sick," I said and chucked a pen at him.

Nathan caught it and licked the tip.

I quirked my brow at him. "Did you learn that trick from Tiffany?"

"No, I learned that one from you this morning, watching you on your knees in the shower with my hands guiding your whore of a mouth." He laughed when I swallowed hard and gave him a warning look.

"I'm serious, Nathan. Owen's really been helping out around here. It makes me feel safer. I wish there was a way I could thank him."

"Well, you're not giving him the guy's version of flowers, if that's what you're thinking." He smirked.

I sighed. "Always thinking with your cock."

"Always thinking about your cunt," he corrected me.

"Who's cunt?" Andrew's voice said before we saw him appear in our office.

"The one you need. Go find your own," Nathan said and chucked the pen at him, the one he licked.

"Gross!" I said under my breath.

"It's just a word for pussy," Nathan said, teasing me.

"The things you guys talk about during work hours." Andrew rolled his eyes and shook his head.

"Yeah, and you wish you had it." Nathan chuckled and leaned back in his chair, looking pleased with himself.

"Is there a reason you're here?" I asked Andrew. "I mean, I know you two are buddies again, but you know Nathan doesn't really like you hanging around me a lot."

Andrew winked, then closed the door. "I know. I just stopped by to tell bozo here you guys need to be more careful. Jennifer's spreading rumors about you two."

I rolled my eyes and groaned.

"And it's not pretty," Andrew added.

"That's because it's coming out of her. Pretty and Jennifer don't mix," Nathan said. He gripped the back of his neck.

"What's she saying now?" I leaned forward in my seat.

"Actually, I phrased it wrong. She's saying that you, Lila, have been coming on to Owen; that she's pretty sure she saw you both kissing in your office. I think she's trying to get you and Owen fired so she can have Nathan all to herself." Andrew pointed at Nathan. "I'm thinking it's because she's caught on that you two are interested in each other, so she's doing what she can to get rid of the competition."

"Shit. She knows I'm interested? But Owen's not even my usual type—I figured no one would pick up on the sexual tension," Nathan deadpanned. "He's not as tall and handsome as you are, Drew." He batted his lashes like a dork.

They both laughed, but the knot in my stomach prevented me from doing more than smile a little. Shit. We were failing in the acting department. It was getting harder every day to keep from showing on my face exactly how much I adored Nathan and how much he meant to me.

A few long days later, I returned home after work and moved to the kitchen to see what I had available to make for dinner, knowing Nathan would be here soon. There was also a chance he would have Andrew in tow, so I needed to find something that was enough to feed four to five people. I pulled out some ingredients to make a salad and chicken to cook up. There was always something to make with chicken.

I was contemplating a side dish or two when I was interrupted by a knocking at the door. My brow scrunched in curiosity as to why Nathan was knocking.

"Why aren't you using your key?" I asked as I walked to

the door, shaking my head and smiling. His hands were probably just full of something.

My hand twisted the knob and swung the door open. I was about to tease him for not being able to open it on his own, or something to that effect, but was stopped by the person on the other side.

My smile faded, my eyes widened, and terror filled my being.

"Long time no see, sis," Adam said from the other side of the threshold.

A DAM FOUND ME.

Adam was in my doorway, standing much closer than the restraining order I once had on him ever allowed.

In that second of recognition I hated the judge, who decided four years without contact from him was enough for it to be lifted. I always knew it was nothing more than a threat, but I also knew that, with its protection, I could have him arrested if he ever came near me.

But that no longer mattered. What did matter was that he was standing at my door, and I was alone. His figure seemed to take up the bulk of the door frame, standing over six feet. He'd grown since I last saw him. Everything else was the same: brown hair, brown eyes, and a hatred for me.

After he spoke, it only took a fraction of a second for my arm to swing the door back in his face. Inches before the door seated, Adam's arm and foot stopped any progression. He pushed back, hard, and I stumbled from the force.

I'd taken self-defense classes long ago, but they could never have prepared me for the emotional response I would have to seeing him again. A feeling of absolute dread, which I hadn't felt in over ten years, took hold, clouding my mind, and I couldn't remember anything.

He stepped inside and slammed the door behind him, his arm reaching out and locking the deadbolt. I searched around, frantic for something, anything I could use as a weapon or throw at him. Running was no good; he was standing between me and the only way out.

My panic rose, calling out Nathan's name in my mind over and over again, as if he might hear my distress. I didn't even have my phone on me, so there was no way to call for help. All of it was futile anyway because Adam was on a mission, and I knew he was unstoppable when he was determined to do something. He stepped toward me, and I fruitlessly stepped back.

"What are you doing here, Adam?" I was trying to stall what I could feel coming before I reminded him. "You're not allowed to be anywhere near me."

His eyes became slits, his muscles clenching, the hatred rolling off of him. I was crumpling inside against it, just as I did when I was younger.

"Oh, no, little sis. It's been almost ten years since that stain was removed. However, this one," he sneered, pointing to me, "still remains."

I swallowed hard. "You need to leave."

He laughed at me. "Leave? Oh, I think not. Do you have any idea the damage you caused, you little fucking bitch?"

My body shook as I inched back, but his eyes were trained on my every move.

"I was the victim."

"You fucking asked for it," he spat. "You know, in a small

town, gossip spreads. Like wildfire. When I returned to school the Monday after the court ruling, everyone knew. You fucking aired our dirty laundry, made yourself out to be some fucking helpless little girl and me out to be a monster!"

He lashed out, his hand grabbing at the decorative vase on the entry table and hurtling it across the room. It shattered against the wall, and I jumped, my chest tightening. I was scared and saw no hope of the situation ending well. I owned a gun, but it did me no good thirty feet away in the bedroom with a lock on it and unloaded. There was no way I would have the time to get to it and get it prepped.

"Girls don't like guys who are described as monsters, Delilah." He took slow, meticulous steps toward me. "Adults don't like thugs, and colleges don't like guys who already have restraining orders against them and are in anger management courses. I was labeled a bad seed."

"You *are* a bad seed," I whispered, trying to stand up to him, but knowing he physically would crush me, just as he was emotionally.

It didn't matter, because I knew.

Adam was here to kill me.

It wasn't his intent, but there would be no one to stop him this time. My father was always there in the past to make sure it never went that far. After all, he couldn't ruin his reputation with the town by being implicated in any way with the death of his own daughter.

"What the fuck did you say?" There was a burning, furious flame in his eyes.

He stomped toward me, and I tried to step away but his arm swung back and then forward. I managed to dodge his attack, but didn't see when it swung back a second time. The back of his hand collided with my jaw, and I stumbled to the ground.

"It was all your fucking fault! You fucking asked for it!"

The taste of blood invaded my mouth. My mind was screaming at me to run as it mapped out different routes I could maneuver in order to get around him.

Before I was even able to stand, his hand reached out, his large fingers circling around my throat. I clawed at his fingers in an effort to get him to release me. It only made him angrier; he pushed me toward the wall and slammed my head against the mirror that was hanging there.

The sting from the glass shards as they cut into my scalp caused me to scream out. Warm beads of blood began to run down my forehead. My vision distorted for a moment from the blow, and I was having trouble telling how close he was to me.

I didn't waste what little breath I had on screaming. There was no one around to hear me anyway.

"I never did anything," I managed to choke out, stalling again as I tried to find an opening.

"You provoked me, and you know it!" He pushed me harder into the wall. My nails dug into his forearm and hand, but he still wouldn't release my throat. "Always walking around like you were better than me when *you* are nothing."

My breaths were becoming shallow and my vision was beginning to fade. He must have noticed because his grip relaxed. This gave me enough clarity to see the angle of his body. My leg swung out, landing right between his.

He howled in pain before pulling me away from the wall and throwing me down to the ground, venom spitting from his lips. "Fucking worthless cunt! You'll pay for that."

I coughed on the ground as I tried to regain my breath, but

I didn't get very much time before his boot collided with my stomach. I cried out in pain, stars dancing across my eyes, and begged for him to stop.

"Stop? Oh no. You made my life a living hell. You took everything away from me, and I'm here to repay you." He delivered another swift kick.

I screamed in pain, curling up into a ball and whimpering. Tears spilled from my eyes. I was no match for him.

I'm sorry, Nathan. I love you.

His footsteps grew closer, so close I heard his rapid breaths. I opened my eyes and watched him squat on the floor next to my head. He grabbed hold of my hair and pulled, maneuvering me until we were eye to eye.

All I saw was an animal playing with its prey, bent on tearing me apart, breaking me before delivering the final blow.

"I saw you in the ally in Noblesville," he said through clenched teeth. My eyes widened. "You were sucking that guy's cock before he fucking rammed it inside you. You were moaning like the whore I always knew you were. You always acted like such a prude, but I knew you couldn't wait for some dick. *My* dick."

His gaze moved down my body, his tongue peeking out to wet his lips. My panic rose. Killing me was one thing. I always knew if I died by the hands of another, it would be Adam. Raping me before he finished me off was something that had never entered my mind.

My legs began to kick and my hands scratched at his, trying to get him to release my hair.

It worked, and I scrambled to get up and away. I only got one step before he grabbed my ankle, and I fell back down to the floor.

"No!" I tried to kick him off as he pinned me down.

I managed to get one punch across his face, but it wasn't enough for him to even notice. I thought I was gaining traction, my screams deterring him. Then his fist met my face, and I quieted down.

I still pushed against him, still fought. I would never let him have me. I would die before I let that happen.

There was a tug at my chest; it was followed by the ping of the buttons from my blouse, plinking on the hardwood floor. I reached up and scratched his face, breaking skin and leaving trails that began to seep blood.

"You fucking bitch!" He grabbed the sides of my face and slammed my head into the floor. His hand trapped my wrists and pinned them above my head.

My head lolled, my mind fighting for balance in the spinning room.

He reached down to the hemline of my skirt, and I shrieked, my legs kicking wildly. "No. No! Stop! No, no, no. Don't!"

It didn't deter him, and his hand continued its way up, pushing my skirt up my thighs.

My hips tried to buck him off, while my legs kicked, trying to squirm away. My heart was racing and my vision was blurring. At that rate I was going to blackout before he killed me, never knowing if he raped me before I died.

There was a growling sound and air whooshing past as the weight and hands that had me pinned down were removed.

My head moved to the side, and in my blurry vision, I saw two people fighting. The sound of flesh hitting flesh filled my ears.

"Lila!" a familiar voice called out.

Andrew was leaning over me, and the struggle that was across the room was escalating.

"I'm okay," I managed to croak.

He nodded, then headed over to the two fighting figures. Nathan was cussing before each crunch, and I knew he had the upper hand.

"Enough!" Andrew said. "I've got him. Go to her!"

There was a grumble of defeat from what I knew was Adam and watched the figure get up and run to me before Andrew sat down on Adam's stomach.

Adam groaned from Andrew's weight.

"Keep it up, asshole. I'm more than happy to pick up where Nathan left off." Andrew slammed his fist into Adam's face when he tried to punch him. Adam howled in pain.

Nathan ran toward me, a loud gasp escaping him as he took in my appearance before he fell to the floor beside me.

"Lila, baby, are you all right? Oh, God, you're bleeding…*a lot*," Nathan said in a panic, his fingers ghosting over my skin.

I smiled up at him, my head leaning into his touch as the tears fell from my eyes. "You came, you made it."

"Always. I'll always protect you." His voice was wavering. A tear slid down his face and landed on my cheek, making my heart clench for him. "I can't lose you."

"I was so scared!" I cried out and began sobbing, my fingers clenching around the fabric of his jacket.

Nathan leaned down and scooped me up into his arms. "I know, Honeybear. I'm here now, I've got you. He won't hurt you again, I promise."

There was an edge in his voice, and I believed him. Nathan would do anything to protect me. Andrew's voice rang around the walls as he contacted 911 and then called down to the front desk to inform Mike of their imminent arrival.

I started to shake, the shock of everything settling in.

"I'm so sorry I wasn't here earlier." Nathan kissed my forehead while his fingers stroked my hair.

My eyes closed as I hummed in reaction to the comfort that helped me to forget about the pain I was in. His lips lightly brush mine, and I smiled.

"Move in with me," he said suddenly, and my eyes fluttered open as I tried to focus on him.

"What?" I was confused by not only the question, but the timing.

"We already spend every night with each other, why have two places? Plus, I would feel better knowing you're as safe… well, as safe as you can be with me."

It made sense. He hadn't been to his place in months, and I had a feeling I wouldn't want to stay here anymore.

"Okay."

"Okay? You're not going to fight with me on this?" Shock of my acceptance was evident on his features.

I shook my head, but stopped when it felt like my brain was jiggling. "You're right, and I want to live with you Nathan. I love you."

"I love you, too," he replied and kissed me again, this time a little deeper. "Now if I can just keep you out of the hospital, we'll be in good shape."

"It's not my fault," I said in protest, my vision starting to dim as I shook. Tears spilled from my eyes, the pain growing immense.

"I know. It never was yours, baby. It was always his." Nathan placed a kiss on my forehead again while his fingers stroked down my arm.

My eyes widened in fear at the figure that burst through the door, his forceful entrance made my heart rate spike. I was starting to hyperventilate, the room getting darker when my vision cleared.

The man's facial expression was not of anger, but horror. Noah.

Noah was standing in front of me—the boy who'd also had a terrible childhood. The boy I'd once been afraid of after being freed from the nightmare that was my father's home. The kind boy who helped me learn not all men were monsters and some were even good. He was here, and I was safe.

My eyes rolled back and the world faded away.

My mind became aware before my eyes were willing to open. There was a throbbing—no, *slamming*—pain in my head. It hurt to breathe a bit, but not in my chest or ribs. Lower, like in my stomach. I began to wonder why when the events rushed back into my mind.

It was all pain from my injuries. Proof I was alive, that Adam didn't kill me, and Nathan made it in time.

My eyes fluttered open to find Nathan staring down at me. He let out a sigh of relief and squeezed my hand.

"How long have I been out?" I asked, noticing I was in yet another hospital room. Three times in six months had to be a record of some sort.

"We just got here a few minutes ago," Nathan said. Andrew was also in the room, standing guard over us. "So, not too long."

I looked around more and gasped before my vision focused on the figure of the cop standing a few feet from me. He hadn't changed since I last saw him: still tall with brown hair and matching eyes. His nose still crooked from when his father broke it.

"Noah?" I nodded, giving him our customary symbol that he was okay to approach, and he rushed over to my side.

He took my hand in his. "How are you feeling?"

"Been better, been worse." I gave a gentle shrug, knowing he understood. I tried not to think about what had happened. I was used to hiding the pain after an attack, but it had been so long.

It was surreal chatting with Noah like we were seated on my couch. The whole situation would be frightening if it weren't for Nathan, Andrew, and Noah's comforting presence.

I was safe.

Adam would be hauled off like a wild animal to be caged as he should've been years ago. Deep down I knew that between Noah, Nathan, and Andrew, justice would be served. I blinked hard and honed in on Noah's words to keep myself centered and calm. If I was calm, Nathan would be as well.

"I called you a few months ago, but you didn't call back. I've been worried something like this had happened to you." Noah's laid back voice was what I needed.

"I'm sorry, so sorry. I didn't mean to worry you. It's been… hectic this year." I was kicking myself for not calling him.

"Well, besides the blood and fat lip, you're looking good, kid." His smile was good-natured and warmed me.

"You, too. That uniform looks good on you. Your mom would be proud to see her son protecting people and putting the bad ones in jail." I tried not to cringe; the pain in my back and head was starting to throb. My bones ached, but inside I felt so happy for so many things. Happy that Andrew was my friend and here for me, that Adam was history. But most of all, happy Nathan and I were together. Nothing would come between us.

"Thank you, Lila. That means a lot." His eyes misted as he smiled at me.

"How's Camilla?"

"She's good. Wants you to come out and see the girls. They've gotten so big since you saw them at Christmas, you'd be amazed." He beamed down at me.

"I'm so sorry. I should have kept better contact," I said, apologizing again.

"It's okay. I can see something big has happened since I last saw you. You'll have to come over for dinner soon and bring this guy with the heavy fists with you." He pointed to Nathan.

"Oh…Nathan, this is Noah Hanson. Noah, this is Nathan Thorne."

"Pleasure to meet you. Lila's told me a lot about you." Nathan held out his hand for Noah who took it.

Noah held a questioning gaze. "Thorne? Former prosecutor Thorne?"

Nathan blinked at him. "Yes."

Noah tensed, his eyes flickering to the wall that held the door and window before his eyes locked with Nathan's. "You need to come to dinner with Lila."

Nathan nodded, and they did one of those guy exchange things before letting go. I was certain Nathan would explain it to me later; there was some undertone conversation I missed. With the way my head was still pounding, I was certain an elephant could run through the room, and I wouldn't notice.

"Well, I need to get back to work. We need to take a couple pictures of your injuries, okay? Then you'll need to answer some more questions for the report."

I nodded in response, and Noah turned to leave.

"Noah!" I called out, and he turned back. "Could you call Teresa and Armando, tell them what happened, and that I'm all right?"

"They're already in the waiting room; I called them right after you passed out, but I'll let them know. Get better and give me a call soon." He waved as he walked out of the room and past the cops guarding the door.

On his way out, I watched as Adam was wheeled down the hall, handcuffed to a gurney. His face was swollen, and blood was still oozing out of his nose as well as the two places where his lips were split. He was groaning in pain.

I smiled a bit, happy to see him get a small taste of his own medicine. I took Nathan's hands in mine and pulled them to where I could see. His knuckles were swollen and a few were bleeding a little.

"Thank you," I whispered as I pulled his hand to my lips, placing light kisses on each knuckle. "All that practice on your walls paid off."

He leaned down and kissed me. "Always, Honeybear."

The doctors came in and began running me through the exam, followed by tests and machines to make sure I had no internal bleeding from Adam's vicious kicks. They also wanted to make sure there was no damage done to my skull and brain.

I loved having Nathan near. I needed him; he kept me calm, kept the shaking at bay. Though, every time I looked at him, tears sprung to my eyes. I was almost taken from him. His own look of fright was so overwhelming I didn't know what to do to calm him because they kept him more than an arm's length away so they could work.

Nurses took him away for his own exam and to clean off

his wounds, but they returned him as soon as possible. Andrew went to the waiting room to sit with Teresa and Armando.

The police came in between tests to get my statement, and I found it was difficult to recount the details to them. Nathan erupted in a fit of rage as I divulged the first few moments after I opened the door, and he had to be escorted out for the remainder of their inquisition.

I began vibrating, tears flowing as I let my mind think about it. I told them what I could remember; some things were hazy, though, due to trauma he inflicted to my head. They took a few photos of my injuries, and then said they'd be back in a day or two for more information, before they left.

The hospital decided to keep me overnight for observation. Another concussion, but the rest was superficial. I was bruised and a few deep cuts from the glass of the mirror were stitched up. Everyone in the waiting room was sent home. I couldn't see anyone; I only needed Nathan at that moment. I was fighting to keep my eyes open, but through the glass I saw Nathan talking to Teresa, her arms wrapped around him, sobs racking her body before the darkness took over and I was shut away from the world.

MY EYES FLUTTERED OPEN, AND I SIGHED AT THE CLOCK ON the wall, telling me it was only three in the morning. There was a weight in my hand, and I looked down to find Nathan asleep, his head resting on the bed, one hand in mine. His hands were bandaged, and I knew his neck had to be killing him from the angle.

Lifting my free hand, I ran my fingers thought the silky strands of his hair. I took stock of my aches while I soothed myself by touching him. My neck was in immense pain when I moved it, so much that it was difficult to look down at him. Adam's fingers bruised the muscle. My face was swollen in multiple places, giving me that beach ball like feeling again, and the taste of rust was on my tongue from the large split in my lip. I could feel the location of several places they stitched back together in my scalp and at my hairline. I clenched the muscles of my stomach and instantly regretted it.

All in all, I came out better than I had most of the other times. It was, for the most part, superficial. Painful, but it would all heal. No broken bones, torn muscles, or dislocated anything this time. It was all due to Nathan. *If he hadn't come…if he hadn't made it…*

Tears filled my eyes, and I tried to keep the sob in, knowing if Nathan had been as little as five more minutes, I would be in a different part of the hospital—the part people went into once.

"Lila?" Nathan's rough, groggy voice asked; his fingers reached up to wipe away my tears.

"I didn't want to leave you!" I cried out unexpectedly, the tears now streaming down my face. He grabbed my hand and buried his face in it, gripping it with his own. Wet drops landed on my skin, tearing at my heart.

"I was so scared, Honeybear. I heard your screams as soon as the door of the elevator opened. My heart stopped, baby, and I ran as fast as I could to find you. I thought it was the Marconi. When I opened the door…" His body shuddered at the memory, his grip on my hand tightening. His eyes were squeezed shut, jaw clenched. "I wanted to fucking kill him. I wanted to rip his arms off and shove them down his fucking throat for even touching you. I wanted him dead for hurting you."

I pulled in a shuddering breath, willing myself to calm down so that I could tell him. I needed to tell him.

"That was the first time I ever tried to fight back," I whispered. "Before…before, it would just make him even angrier and hit me harder. There was no escape back then. This time, though, I knew. He was there to kill me, Nathan." My voice cracked at the end, my bottom lip trembling as tears continued to spill down my cheeks. "He was there to kill me, but he got…distracted."

I could say it in my head, but I couldn't say what he was about to do out loud. Nathan understood, his hand reaching up and persuading me to look at him. His eyes held a furious fire, his body vibrating in anger.

"He will never fucking touch you again. He will never be anywhere near you unless it's in the courtroom. I will do everything in my power to make damn certain that fucker never breathes free air again."

I believed him, and I held a desperate hope he could. The accusations tolled up in my head, but would they be enough to lock him away for good? Nathan had done the impossible with one of the Marconi, putting them away, but would he be successful when my family was involved? And could he do this without putting himself back in harm's way by bringing attention to where he was? It was all too frightening and overwhelming to think about, and the scariest thing of all was I knew he'd do this for me without sparing it a second thought. I knew his natural inclinations as a damn fine, unstoppable lawyer would kick in. Would I be able to stop him if he set his mind to do it?

Nathan let go of my hand and wrapped his arms around me. My security blanket. In an instant I felt calmer, and placed a kiss on his neck, but the tears still trickled down.

"I love you, so much." I needed him to know as I fisted my hands in his shirt.

"Not as much as I love you," he replied, kissing my lips.

Not long after, Nathan crawled up onto the narrow hospital bed at my urging. His arms wrapped around me and we both drifted back off to sleep.

Rules were meant to be broken. Nobody knew that better than us.

A few short hours later, the bed stirred and my eyes opened. He gave me an apologetic look as he gathered his things.

I sighed, knowing he couldn't miss work as well; it would raise too many suspicions. How much longer would we put up with all the pretenses? How much longer would we suffer being so close, yet so far away from one another?

He gave me a sound kiss, told me he loved me, and he would see me soon. My hand stretched out as he stepped away, not wanting to let go of his. I knew he wanted to stay, but we both knew why he had to go. He also had to leave so he could tell Jack what happened and that I wouldn't be in.

I was released a few hours later, Teresa and Sarah teaming up to take me home. It was difficult to walk, hunched over from the pain in my stomach. Doctor's orders had me resting for the remainder of the week.

Everything was fine as we rode in the elevator and walked down the hall. Though as soon as the door opened, I couldn't enter. The evidence was still there: crime scene tape, the shattered vase and mirror. I started hyperventilating as memories of the attack crashed down on me, and I stumbled back out into the hallway wall.

"I can't, I can't," I pleaded and they both understood, shutting the door.

Teresa rushed over to me, wrapping her arms around me and whispered soft words. "It's okay. You don't ever have to go back in there if you don't want to. We'll take care of everything."

I couldn't explain my reaction; it was so strange. When I was younger I was used to going back to the scene of the crime, because it was home, and I had no other choice. But for some reason, it was different. Maybe because I was so certain I was going to die. Or maybe it was because I had made this home my sanctuary, my safe place, and Adam had come in and destroyed that within a matter of moments. All I knew was I couldn't go back in.

Taking my hand, they helped me up to Nathan's condo, and I settled into his bed. I was hoping for his scent to be lingering on the pillows and sheets to help soothe me, but it'd been so long since he'd slept there, any trace of him had faded. Months spent in my condo left his empty of a presence I needed.

Moving to the dresser, I pulled out one of his Harvard shirts that hadn't made their way down to my place and slipped it on. I needed to be near him in any way that I could.

He was my safe place now—my sanctuary I could always turn to.

I awoke to soft, gentle kisses, feather light against my skin. My eyes strained against the light in the room, the angle of the sun telling me it was sometime around noon. I didn't even realize I'd fallen asleep.

"Nathan?" My eyes searched out where the kisses were taking place, wondering what he was doing home.

My head turned and there he was, staring down at me with trepidation in his eyes. "How are you feeling, Honeybear?"

"I'm…I have no answer besides happy you're here. What are you doing here?"

"I'm having lunch."

My brow scrunched. "What are you having?"

"I was hoping for some lovey hugs. I have a desperate need for them."

My hands wound around his neck while his wrapped around my body. "I need them, as well."

Our time was short, lying there touching and caressing. It was what we both needed, a connection to the other. To feel each other and know the other was alive.

Tender touches, soft kisses, and tears. Everything was so raw and fresh, and I knew we needed to see Dr. Morgenson before the day was over.

Darren came over as soon as Nathan arrived home after work. We moved into the bedroom so that I could lie down. Sarah left with a promise that she would be back the next day.

As soon as we were in the room, I had an indescribable need to tell Dr. Morgenson, and Nathan, a detailed description of what happened. It was like I was purging the images from my mind by putting them into words. Somehow it was more real, I wasn't making it up. They would believe me; there was no one there to discredit me.

No tears spilled as I spoke. I felt like I was having a strange, out-of-body experience as I recounted the gory details.

Nathan couldn't stay with me on the bed; he was distressed hearing all that occurred. His hands were pulling at his neck as he paced.

There was a loud crunching sound as I described the end when he was trying to rape me. Nathan had punched the wall, splintering the drywall.

Somehow, with everything that happened, all I could think was "Oh, Erin is going to kill you." How odd. Was I used to being attacked, or had I cracked again and didn't know it?

Nathan was hanging his head and berating himself.

Darren managed to get through to him, and he returned to me. The doctor also told him he'd deal with Nathan's wall punching habit very soon. Granted, it was the first time in months it had happened.

I went back to telling them what had taken place. The tears had started when I began talking about the end. All I could think of was my last thought for Nathan, begging his forgiveness for dying.

"I want to pull you inside me so you're safe," he said as he climbed back onto the bed and wrapped his body around mine.

"This attack was different. You've always had such a hard time talking about them, but this one is pouring out of you. Why do you think that is?" Darren asked.

"Because I knew there was no one to stop him…that I was going to die. At the same time, though, I fought back. I didn't take it like when I was younger. I have a reason to live now, and in some weird, sick way, I feel safe. He's not coming back this time; he's no longer hiding in the shadows. I know where he is and in the place he's being held, he can't hurt me anymore. I'm no longer alone with no one to protect me. I have Nathan. I have Andrew and Caroline. I have so many people now that I didn't have before. So, in a way, this was a good thing."

Nathan, Andrew, and Caroline filled me in on the staff meeting that occurred the day after my incident with Adam. Jack had to let everyone know why I was out. He left out the details, but they knew I'd been attacked and would be out.

Jack knew and respected my privacy about my past, and left off that it was someone I knew and in my own home. They warned me about the looks I would receive, looks that would be different than the ones from my accident.

I returned to work after the weekend, bruises on full display, but a scarf around my neck to hide the perfect print of Adam's hand around it. The marks had faded, but only some. My lip was healing, but the split was still obvious. There was still a large purple bruise on my cheekbone that makeup couldn't hide.

Andrew was waiting for me when I got off the elevator to escort me to my office. I gave him a hug in thanks, trying to convey how grateful I was for his friendship and support.

The looks of pity came after the gasps and stunned looks as their eyes took me in, all thinking about how sad it was after all I'd already been through. It was unnerving when random coworkers came up and hugged me. I could handle my friends and family hugging me, but random people still made me uneasy and I froze, wide-eyed. I was grateful that every time it happened, Caroline or Andrew was around. Even Owen could see how uncomfortable it made me and had people back off.

I hated the attention, and it was wearing me down. Coffee was needed, though as I walked into the break room, I knew it wouldn't end well. My strange elation of the breaking of the chains that bound me to Adam combined with all the touching had me in a whole new mental state.

I should've known Jack's announcement wouldn't break through the self-centered skulls of Nathan's fan club. I had no idea what their problem was with me, but I was getting sick of it. Maybe Andrew was right to worry—maybe Jennifer *did* suspect something was going on with Nathan and me.

"Out again, Lila?" Jennifer snapped as soon as I had one foot in the room.

"Have a nice vacation while we were all working?" Kelly sneered.

Did none of them pay attention to Jack? Or was it because it was about me, so they ignored it?

"Vacation? Well, if you call getting attacked, nearly raped, and almost killed in my own home a vacation, then it was fucking peachy!" I spat at them, glaring. Were they so blinded by their self-centeredness that they didn't see my injuries? Everyone else tried not to stare, but failed. Yet they didn't even notice.

Jennifer rolled her eyes. "Are you that desperate for attention?"

"I bet she's hoping to get a sympathy screw," Tiffany said with a laugh. "That'd be like you. Did you fall down the stairs or something?"

I pulled the scarf from my neck, exposing the handprint bruise that covered my skin before pulling my hair back to expose the stitches. I heard them gasp. "The only thing I'm desperate for is for you to leave me the fuck alone. I've never done anything to you; I'm no threat to you. Stop fucking bullying me, because I have lived with it enough in my life and last week it almost killed me. So, shut the fuck up and stop pissing on people to make yourselves feel better!" I raged, slapping the file out of Kelly's arms as I pushed past them to the coffee maker.

Andrew was coming in from the other entrance and a smile spread on his face. He threw a questioning look in my direction.

"Nothing to worry about. The stupid bitches aren't worth my time."

He chuckled at me as he poured the coffee, handing me a cup.

It became obvious that Nathan was rubbing off on me.

And I was learning to fight back.

Things seemed to move on fast forward, our days even more crammed than before. We were becoming lax, careless. The masks we once kept in tight check began to slip once again.

Evidence came spilling in after Adam's attack, making our case stronger with each person Noah talked to. He called a few days after and told us a woman close to Adam said he had become agitated after he saw me in the alley, chanting he was going to "kill the fucking bitch." She even said she thought Adam might've recorded me with his phone when he saw me. I shuddered to think that might possibly be true.

I learned how he found out where I was: it was due to the shop I admired so much. I'd put my address down for mailings because I wanted to be informed when they had sales.

I should have known better, being that close.

Noah found evidence that indicated Adam had been following me for a few days. Somehow, he never made the connection of Nathan and me though, or that Nathan was the one from the alley.

Mike, the door guard, apologized over and over for letting him get the better of him. Adam had caused a distraction, allowing him to slip past Mike's careful watch. The security cameras caught everything, and I tried to let Mike know I didn't blame him. He still took it pretty hard though. The man took pride in his job.

The property manager wanted to discipline him, and I begged him not to. There was no reason to; he already felt bad enough. It didn't matter who was on watch that day, Adam was going to get through. Even if he had to beat the guard down.

It was moving day, and I was happy to never have to return to my condo after the weekend. It'd been ten days since Adam attacked me, but many of the marks still remained. My condo no longer held its marks, with the exception of a few scratches in the hardwood from the glass of the vase he'd thrown. Sarah and Teresa had gone in and cleaned everything, but I found some things couldn't be scrubbed clean. Like the memories.

While there, they brought up most of my clothes and helped to rearrange Nathan's closet in order to fit everything. His suits took up a lot of room and a few items were moved into one of the extra bedrooms. Nathan retrieved anything else I needed before moving day, and we drew up a game plan to merge my belongings in with his.

The lack of furniture and decorations made the decision much easier. When they were fixing the walls and repainting Nathan's condo, Sarah and Erin had begged to decorate, but Nathan was against it. Even then he knew we would move in together one day, or at least hoped, so he didn't see the need. My armoire would be moved into the master bedroom, while the rest of the bedroom furniture and my guest room items were moved into the two empty bedrooms. My office was to be moved and merged in with his. So on and so forth.

Entering my condo, crossing the threshold, was the easy part. Shutting the door and being surrounded by the stifling air was the hard part. I made it through, but the toll it took on me was staggering.

I was fine as long as I wasn't in that area. He only tainted the space around the entry and the fond memories I had with Nathan there. Calm filled me in my bedroom, but there was also a little bit of sadness. Much of my relationship with Nathan happened within the expanse of those walls, some of my happiest times. I'd never felt attached to my home until he came into my life.

A few times I needed to go to the entry, to answer the door, take a box up, and each time, my pace picked up. The longer I was in the space, the more I was haunted by the memories.

I thought I was okay, that I beat down my demons, but Adam marked more than my skin. Even Nathan's touch wasn't the same, and I hurt him, pushed him away. He understood, and was taking things slower.

By noon I was running through the entry, feeling as if a phantom was waiting to grab me if I lingered too long. Nathan caught me, halting me on my fourth pass, and I was afraid to meet his gaze.

"Honeybear, please look at me." My head rose, and the worried look of pain on his face caused my heart to clench. "Are you sure you're okay?"

I looked over my shoulder and shook my head. His arms wrapped around me, drawing me close. I relaxed then, his presence so soothing.

"I keep remembering every time I'm in that area. I know I said I was all right, and it did feel good to tell you everything, but still… I can't shake the feelings it evokes. I can almost feel his fingers wrap around my neck, squeezing so hard I can't breathe. The back of his hand as it came down across my face. The sheer terror that he was going to rape me, and those would be my last memories."

Nathan's grip tightened, and he was shaking. "He'll never touch you again." His voice was strained. "I'm going to work with the prosecutor's office to make sure of that. If I can get a Marconi imprisoned, I can get him put away for life."

I pulled back and looked up at him. Determination and anger flickered in his eyes. This was exactly what I was afraid of.

"That's more than just helping out. Do you… Are you ready for that? To return to the courtroom? Would they even let you help in that capacity? It would put you in danger, wouldn't it?"

"Free consultant in the form of a former Federal Prosecutor? I hope they wouldn't pass that up. It'll be fine." His hands rubbed up and down my arms.

I let out a shuddering breath. "I just… It worries me."

He bent down, his lips kissing at my worry lines. "What is this about?"

"I don't want you to get hurt because of me."

His brow scrunched. "That's my line. Are you the one thinking about the Marconi family this time?" I nodded and he sighed, pulling me back to his chest and kissing the top of my head. "I won't tell you it hasn't crossed my mind, but your safety is more important than my own. I need to do this. I wasn't there to protect you from him, so I'll protect you by making sure he doesn't even have the opportunity to do it again."

"You couldn't have known—there was no way." I shuffled around a bit, uneasy at the thought of him being a target. My jaw tightened, and a pang in my chest made me feel slightly hollow. I wanted to keep him safe with me.

"He tried to take you from me. I want to kill him with my bare hands for that, but that would take me from you, so this is what I do." His voice was imploring me to understand.

"I get that."

"But?" he pressed.

"There are things I'm afraid of."

"*Things?*"

I pursed my lips. "First, I know how upset you get when I tell you about the past. In order to do this, you'll need to pull information from back then to show his history of violence. Second, what if…what if I see my father and Cheryl?"

"I'm sorry," he whispered against my forehead with a sigh.

"For what?"

"I hadn't even thought about what this will do to you. You're right; we'll have to show a history of violence to help put him away for good."

"All of the charges along with the evidence are enough to keep him there for a while. Thank God he didn't have the money to make bail and will be in jail for the months before the trial, but that will be needed to drive home the attempted…" my voice trailed off, the word stuck in my throat. Nathan squeezed me tighter. "… murder. That this wasn't a crime of passion, it was premeditated. The evidence Noah found proves that."

"I'm going to push for a jury trial. Not that a judge trial would really hurt due to the evidence we have, but the sympathy from the jurors might help seal the deal. We'll both have to make sure not to miss any sessions with Darren until this is all over. It's going to dig up some major skeletons for you," he said, brushing my hair back from my face.

"Yes, and you know how much I don't like to talk about it. But I think this will be good in the end. Cleansing. Vindicating. I'm going to need a lot of lovey hugs, and I may not be able to ask for them."

He smiled against my neck and chuckled. "I'll make certain you are well supplied."

There was a clearing of throats as we were interrupted; Andrew and Trent wanting to know where the couch was headed. Moving day continued into the night, and by dinnertime it was empty, no trace of me to be found.

As the days passed, I found it harder to convince myself I was okay, that the attack was no different, but things only seemed to get worse.

I awoke unable to breathe, my nightmare following me. Ghostly fingers were wrapped around my neck, and I was gasping, clawing at invisible hands.

The light flipped on and Nathan loomed over me. The images in my mind began to fade, and the tightness lessened. A scream clawed its way out of me, loud and raw.

"Shh, it's okay. I'm here. He can't hurt you," Nathan said as he wrapped his arms around me.

Tears were streaming down my face, and I turned into his chest as a sob ripped from me.

"I've got you, baby. You're safe."

He ran soothing caresses down my back, his touch grounding me to him as it always did. It was the third time in a week I'd woken in that dream.

It took a few minutes, but I was able to calm down, secure

in his arms. He felt so good wrapped around me, and I gave in to the sensation of his skin on mine, the familiar heat from being so close to him was turning me on.

My need to feel more was great. I wanted the mind cleansing that only Nathan could provide.

I tilted my head up and pulled his lips down to mine. It was soft, his mouth traveling around my skin, placing open-mouthed kisses on my neck where the bruises from Adam's hands had been. He was covering the bad touch with a loving and pleasurable one.

It'd been over two weeks since I was attacked, and it was the first time Nathan and I had attempted to be intimate since then. A moan slipped out as he licked up my neck, nipping just behind my ear.

"Fuck, baby, I need you," he whispered into my ear, his hips rocking his cloth-covered cock against my thigh.

His hand slid around the front, mouth on mine as he kissed me harder. It was what I wanted, what I needed; Nathan to consume me.

My hips began to rock in time with his as he pinched my nipple through the cloth of my t-shirt, the fire growing. His chest rumbled, and his grip became harder, his own desires releasing from the chains he'd kept them restrained in.

His hand moved down my side, squeezing my thigh hard before moving back up.

That action sparked an awareness and my mind cleared. My heart began sprinting as a panic set in with each inch his hand crawled up my thigh, pushing up the material of the t-shirt I was wearing.

When his hand reached the top of my thigh, fingers on my panties, I lost it. I screamed out as I pushed on his chest. "No!"

All his movements stopped, and he backed away to look at me. My fear echoed in his eyes.

"Lila?"

A shaky hand rose to my mouth when I realized what I'd done.

"I'm sorry. I'm so sorry," I said as dread and a new wave of sobs washed over me.

His eyes softened, and he leaned forward in a motion to wrap his arms around me. I jumped when he touched me, but melted into his embrace.

I apologized over and over as he held me, still in shock from my reaction. It was Nathan, the man I loved. How could I ever confuse his touch with Adam's?

He wouldn't touch me in an intimate way after that, and after my reaction, I couldn't blame him.

Days later he was staring at me, his hands on either side of me braced on the counter, hovering. His body was shaking with need. We were both frustrated. I frowned up at him, my eyes pleading; he whimpered.

I sighed. "Please?" My fingers knotted in his shirt, trying to pull him to me.

His gaze moved to the floor, his head shaking. "I can't, as much as I want you. I love you too much to hurt you like that again."

My hands slapped flat against his chest. "You didn't hurt me! I didn't panic because of you."

"It was my hand on your skin, Honeybear. You know how I am—I want to touch you in ways that I'm afraid will remind you. I can't stand to see you like that, to have you push me away again."

We were stuck in a standstill. Unable to move forward, and it was hurting us both.

Darren suggested a few exercises that would reintegrate Nathan's touch, to become reacquainted with his naturally aggressive need.

"Touch me," I said.

He had a worried look on his face as his hands trailed up my arms, across my shoulders, and up my neck to cup my face. A small gasp escaped when he passed over my neck as he moved down. His movements faltered, and he stared into my eyes to make sure I was okay. The touch was a light caress as he moved around. With the second pass, he put more pressure behind it.

For two weeks Nathan did that three times a day, each day starting off with a firmer grip.

It worked, because I was standing in the living room panting for him. His hands erased the vile memories on my skin. They were covered with the loving, possessive, passionate, spine-tingling ones of Nathan's.

I jumped on him, sending us crashing to the couch behind him, unable to take any more.

"Oh, fuck, baby, are you sure?" he asked as my mouth ran down his neck, licking and sucking. My fingers searched out the hem of his shirt and pulled it up.

I sat up and looked him straight in the eye. "Nate, if you don't fuck me right now, I'm going to have to take matters into my own hand."

His eyes narrowed, and he bared his teeth at me. "Not going to fucking happen. I make you come. *Me*." His hips flexed up, while his hands pushed my hips down as he slid his cock against my clit.

My head tilted back, and my nipples tightened.

"Then make me." I smiled at him, waiting for him to take the bait and let go on me.

It was euphoric to be rid of the barrier that kept our sexual need locked down.

He grabbed my waist and flipped our positions before pulling both of our shirts off. He wasted no time unbuckling my jeans and pulling them off along with my panties.

The need was too great, so he didn't even bother taking his own off, just pushed them to his knees and settled between my thighs.

My mind was clouded, lost in the lust and feel of Nathan. Only he could make my body sing so much, make me beg for more. The intensity was picking up as the desire grew to uncontrollable proportions, both of us making unintelligible sounds.

"Lila," he growled against my neck, his mouth moving down to the meat of my shoulder, and biting down as he pushed his cock between my slick folds.

The sensation of him filling me cut through the cloud of lust to send flames rushing through my veins. There were no thoughts flittering through my mind, only one word: more.

He gave me more with his hands gripping onto my waist and arms, pinning, moving, pulling.

"Fuck, I've missed this tight little snatch. My dirty girl is so wet for me."

I whimpered, already on edge from his touch and weeks of teasing. With a few more thrusts, I was clenching around him and screaming his name.

His hips jerked, expletives flying from his lips as he let go of weeks' worth of build-up.

"Mine! I'll never let you go," he whispered in my ear through harsh breaths.

I smiled and wrapped my arms around his shoulders. "Yours."

OVER A MONTH HAD PASSED SINCE I STARTED LIVING WITH Nathan, since Adam found me. There were moments when things got tense, and I wasn't sure what do about them. He seemed unsure of what to do about his fears for my safety.

Nathan got to the point where he was paranoid enough he didn't like me going to the grocery store without him, still afraid of what might happen. So, we went together.

"I want some sweet potatoes for dinner," he said as he walked next to me, and we grabbed a cart.

I rolled my eyes and wondered when the sudden penchant for them was coming from. "You don't like sweet potatoes."

"Not the way most people do, but I love them roasted. Chop them up, throw them in some spices and olive oil, and pop them in the oven."

"You sound like quite the cook, but I know better," I teased as we headed to the produce section.

He smirked. "Mom made them for lunch on my birthday one time."

I didn't need to ask which birthday, because the tone in his voice told me all I needed to know. The last one he celebrated.

My eyes were looking around, on guard for any possible person we might know from the office. Nathan seemed much more relaxed about our outing than I thought he should've been, knowing the repercussions.

"Relax," he whispered in my ear and stepped up behind me, placing his hands next to mine on the cart handle. "It's okay, baby, everything is going to be okay. Trust me."

I nodded and leaned back against him.

Maybe it was due to the fact Jack announced the new fraternization policy that week, or the fact that we weren't trying to pretend as much. Either way, I was concerned about getting caught, and what that would mean.

The new policy permitted a relationship between employees now, as long as they worked in different sections of the firm.

Because of the changes set in place, things began to pick up with the Boob Squad. Owen's antagonistic verbal assaults no longer deterred them; as far as they were concerned, there were no more barriers. That meant there was nothing keeping them from Nathan, or him from them. They were all deluded enough to think that if there was no fraternization policy, he would just jump into bed with them.

When Jack made the announcement, it was like watching hungry lions stalking their prey. I felt bad for Nathan, and I wouldn't have laughed if it hadn't been so comical to watch.

A few days later I was walking down the hall, heading to get some water. I passed by the copy room and, in a reflexive move, glanced in. I was met with a shocking sight that took a few moments to register. I backed up and stared hard, unable to take my eyes off the train wreck happening inside.

Poor Nathan was pinned against the copier, trapped by Tiffany. She opened up the top buttons of her shirt and began caressing herself, and she was being none too passive about her actions. She was so short that if he whipped his monster out, she would be titty-fucking him.

I knew it wouldn't happen though. The look on Nathan's face was priceless. If looks could kill…but oh no, she kept advancing. I couldn't help but laugh at his predicament. He was always so polite to them, keeping their advances at bay, but this was getting to be a bit extreme.

I was always the one pissed off when it came to them, him the one laughing at the situation. Oh, how the mighty had fallen, and how the Boob Squad wished he would fall on them.

"Tiffany, you need to back up, now!" Nathan's eyes darted around for something or someone to save him. His grip on the copier made the plastic squeak under the pressure.

"You want this—you want *me*." Her tone was attempting to sound seductive, but came out as desperate. "You know that slut Lila's after you—but I know you're not interested in her. She's so disgusting. She's fucking Owen, and probably fantasizing about you while she does it. Stop pretending you don't want me. I know you do… I see the looks you give me."

I rolled my eyes. She was obviously speaking from her own experience of what was going on in her mind if and when she managed to get laid.

She licked her lips, and Nathan turned pale. She tried to open her shirt more and he attempted to move away.

"And how did you come to this conclusion? Have I ever made an advancement on you? I've never looked at you any differently than I do anyone else that works in this building."

His tone was no longer friendly, but gaining the edge I knew so well. It didn't seem to register to Tiffany though.

She leaned closer, her hands reaching for his and moving it toward her body. "I can see it in your eyes right now, baby. Stop fighting it. You don't have to anymore—the office rules have changed."

Nathan yanked his hand from her grip, glaring at her. "Please stop before you embarrass yourself further or I decide to sue you for sexual harassment."

She stared at him, confusion written on her face. "Sue for sexual harassment?"

"Yes, I've held my tongue all these months, but if your actions continue… You need to stop throwing yourself at me, because I'm never going to touch you. Rebutton your blouse. Now." His tone was cold, jaw tense.

I contemplated interrupting and laying my claim on him or rescuing him, but I was too curious how the train wreck would end. Gawkers' block kept me bolted in place, a front row seat to the show.

She continued to press into him, not swayed by his words, and it was looking grim. Nathan wouldn't hurt a woman. My heart constricted when I considered how opposite he was from Adam, who would batter and torture for his own enjoyment.

"I mean it, Tiffany. Leave now. Do I have to spell it out for you? I. Am. Not. Interested. In. You!" He accentuated the words in the last sentence, practically spitting at her as he spoke, with how angry he'd become.

She gasped in shock. "I knew it! I knew you were a pussy! I told the girls you were…"

"What? *Gay*? Is that what you were going to say?" His eyes were blazing. "God, you are so full of yourself. Let me make this clear. It's not me, it's *you*. *You're* the problem. I do not want you."

With that, he pushed her aside enough to get past while her blouse gaped open after him. I managed to escape before he caught me watching from a distance.

I didn't say anything when we were both back in our office. An hour later, I headed back to the copy room to make the copies I'd originally intended to make when I happened to come across him being cornered by Tiffany.

I grinned as I waited for my copies and was almost skipping my way back to our office. In some ways it had been good to witness without his knowledge how devoted and loyal he was to me. He'd never stray and cheat on me or do anything again to hurt me. These thoughts made my heart swell. I was almost to our door when I stopped and heard him growl, low and menacing.

"Get the fuck off me. Didn't your little friend tell you? I don't want you or your toxic pussy any-fucking-where near me. Do *not* fucking touch me again, understand?" Nathan said, finally at his breaking point with one of them. I assumed it wasn't Tiffany since he already gave her the brush-off.

There was a rustling followed by "asshole" before Jennifer stormed out, almost running into me in her anger. She threw me a nasty look before disappearing around the corner.

"What was that about?" I asked as I entered. Owen snickered behind me at his desk but then broke out into full laughter.

Nathan's jaw was clenched tight, his eyes hard as he stared out the door toward Owen.

"She had the fucking audacity to grab my hand and place it under her fucking skirt! Saying she knew I wanted her, and

I was just too afraid to make a move, but with the new policy, blah blah blah! Jesus—it was sick!"

My eyes were wide as I sat down, tossing the file down on my desk. They were really willing to do anything.

I couldn't help the smirk that formed on my face. "Wow, they're getting bolder. Something in the water?"

"No fucking clue, but I feel disgusting. I need to go run my hand under scalding hot water to try and burn a layer off. I could stand them when they were just around, but now they're crossing a fucking line, and that shit ends now. No more Mister-fucking-nice guy."

I couldn't help the victorious smile that formed on my face. *Mine.*

My smile didn't fade even with him glaring at me. It was his own fault, after all, but I had a feeling, and was looking forward to, the punishment I would receive later. Maybe he wouldn't even wait until five.

He pulled on his tie and raised his brow at me to indicate what was coming my way.

Oh, yes, it was going to be a good evening.

It became Nathan's obsession to find out every tiny detail about Adam he could—his personal mission to make sure he went to jail for a long time. He didn't want Adam to ever leave prison.

Nathan became very needy, always having to know where I was at all times. He risked our exposure daily, not caring that it could cost him seeing me every day if we got caught.

It wasn't even five on a Tuesday afternoon and he had me on the edge of my desk with my skirt hiked up, thighs spread and pounding into me. I tried to be as quiet as I could with him whispering dirty things in my ear, making me want to moan out loud and scream his name when he hit that spot deep inside me over and over again. He shoved my panties in my mouth right as my orgasm hit me, muffling my screams.

We weren't ready to part in the workplace. Not yet.

His need was great, and I didn't need Darren in my head telling me to ask him what was wrong, because I knew. Nathan was still scared at the thought of what would have happened if he had been five minutes later or if he'd stopped for gas that day.

Feeling my skin to his was reassurance I was all right. Seeing me, hearing me, wasn't enough. He needed to feel the heat of my desire, his name slipping from my lips, his eyes locked on mine and his teeth marking my skin. His lips swallowed my cries of pleasure only he could produce from me.

Over the next few days after the desk incident, he started to relax a little. However, office romps of some sort occurred much more often than before.

We spent that weekend knee deep in paperwork and state criminal laws. He was trying to see if the court case that separated me from my father's custody could be used as evidence. The judge who oversaw my case also oversaw my domestic violence case against Adam. He was convicted of a class D felony and spent six months in jail. Nathan wanted to use it, as did Lawrence, the prosecutor assigned to the case. It showed it was not the first time Adam had attacked me, injuring me. We also had copies of the expired restraining orders.

I also learned my father was shunned in the community when the truth came out.

We tried to discover anything and everything we could find

to use against Adam. Stories began to surface: old girlfriends he beat, workplace violence, anger management classes. He said it was my fault for the way his life turned out, but after all that I saw and heard in the past few weeks, I concluded he would have turned out that way regardless of those cases. The truth was there would have been someone else, some other person, probably a woman, he would've abused. Adam was just that fucked up.

"Yes!" Nathan yelled out, scaring me half to death.

I turned to him, his eyes wide and a smile stretching from ear to ear.

"What did you find?"

"I was scared, really scared the worst he'd get was for the attempted rape, but he has a prior felony." Yeah, *me*, but we knew that already. He shook his head, seeming to know what I was thinking. "Not just you. A woman named Marie Valda. He attacked her four years ago. She spent two days in the hospital. Two prior attacks along with this one makes him a habitual offender."

My lips curled up, my smile matching his. Double. It would double the sentence.

Nathan grabbed another book from the pile next to his spot on the couch, still digging in, insatiable at finding all he could. I picked up the one beneath and began combing through it.

About an hour later, I looked over to him from my spot on the floor at the coffee table where I had various books and papers spread out. He looked delicious, lying on the couch in only his flannel lounge pants, one arm propped behind his head, some law book, resting on his chest. He was engrossed, and completely ignoring me.

I was bored; we'd been working so hard, but now I was craving attention. Affections had been taking the backseat to putting Adam away for life. I continued to watch him, his eyes flitting about the page. An idea sparked, and I pulled my t-shirt off and tossed it at him. It left me smirking at him in just my little shorts. It landed on his legs and did not receive the response I was hoping for. He grunted in annoyance and kicked it off, his eyes never leaving the book.

I let out a huff before crawling across the floor, stalking toward him when his eyes snapped to me.

"Lila?"

I gave him a wicked grin and climbed onto the couch, straddling his hips and grabbing the book, tossing it on the floor. Taking his hands in mine, I placed them on my breasts.

"Touch me."

His eyes went wide in shock, but his hands didn't move the way I loved, the way I needed. They were still and lifeless.

I leaned over and kissed him, placing all of the attention back on me and what I needed from him. I placed my hands over his, encouraging him with the movements for him to do something, anything to give me friction and hope of release.

"Please, baby. I can't take it. You look so good, and I want you." I breathed against his mouth, kisses left on his lips to persuade him.

It took a moment, but Nathan finally responded like I hoped he would. He growled and pinched my nipples before sitting up and taking them in his mouth. I shuddered in pleasure as he began to ravage me. His fingers flexed into my flesh, his teeth nipping and pulling on my nipples. My hips rocked against the hardening length beneath me.

"Fuck, baby." His hips flexed up as I pushed down.

I chanted his name, grabbing hold of his hair and pulling his head back to devour his lips. "Take me, please. I need you. Take me."

His eyes darkened to almost black, his grip on me tightening.

"Again," he demanded.

My eyes threatened to roll back, and I moaned. "Take me."

He growled and sat up, spinning me around and pushing me down onto my knees. My shorts and panties where pulled down with so much force I heard the fabric tear at the seams.

Nathan's weight sagged the couch on one side—the hot head of his cock rubbing against the inside of my thigh.

"Is this what you want, slut?" He rocked his hard length against my slit. I wiggled my butt, teasing him, earning a smack against the swell of my ass. "You better answer me or I won't give it to you."

"I didn't ask you to give, I told you to take."

His fingers dug into my hips, and he drew in a shuddering breath.

"Fuck, baby," he groaned, his hips rocking faster. His hand landed against my skin again, and I yelped, my pussy clenching and begging for him. "That's it, fucking naughty girl. Every time my hand comes down, making your ass nice and pink, you soak my cock."

"Who do I belong to?"

His fingers dug deeper into my hips. "Me. You are fucking *mine.*" His teeth nipped at my neck as he pulled my hips back to his.

"Then show me. Show me who owns me and my pussy."

He slammed into me, hard, causing my body to clench and convulse around him. He pulled out and thrust back in, pushing me into the arm of the couch. Setting up a wicked hard, rough pace, he grabbed hold of my hair, swirling it around his hand, and pulled.

"Fucking take it. Take my cock. Your pussy loves it, doesn't it?"

I moaned, unable to form a coherent thought. His hand smacked down on my skin as his hand pulled harder on my hair.

"Answer me!"

"Yes, yes! Fucking God, yes, my pussy loves your cock." The whole experience was more intense than any in almost two months. I couldn't even think, wrapped in his overwhelming need and dominance.

I begged for more, and he gave me what I asked for. Harder, rougher, faster. It was instinctual, primal fucking, and I loved every moment.

Over and over he pushed me, until I was a blubbering mess from coming so many times in a row. My body was limp, and he was still pounding into me. Incoherent words fell from his lips, his movements becoming erratic until he let go, spilling inside me.

He collapsed down onto my back, and together we slid down to the couch on our sides. His arms wrapped around me, his hot breath on my neck.

"Damn, Honeybear."

I giggled, the laughter shaking my body. "What?"

"You're going to kill me if you keep that up. Though no better way than balls deep in your pussy…or mouth, or ass. I'm not picky." He chuckled while placing a kiss to my temple.

We both began to laugh, snuggled together in a mass of limp-noodle limbs. Nathan forgot about the book I'd tossed aside and kept me wrapped in his embrace. His fingers caressed and tickled me, making me squirm against him.

We stayed snuggled on the couch for the remainder of the day. Nathan threw the blanket from the back of the couch onto us to keep warm. The TV was on, Sunday movies playing, while we napped on and off.

It was an enjoyable day, and we were well rested for the week to come.

THE DAY STARTED OFF LIKE ANY OTHER MORNING OF LATE: faltering masks and blurred indifference.

Sometime during mid-morning, Libby, the receptionist, knocked on our door.

"There's someone here to see you," she said and stepped aside.

Behind her stood a short man who was less than memorable. His voice, however, was unforgettable: deep baritone that resonated on the walls, and much louder than I expected from his small frame.

"Delilah Palmer? Nathan Thorne?"

"Yes?" We moved from our desk to stand in front of him.

He held out an envelope to each of us.

"You have both been served with a subpoena by the defense attorney."

My eyes grew wide, my gaze flickering to just outside the door and the few gawkers we had developed. While I was looking, Andrew appeared in the doorway.

"Can you tell Lawrence to call me beforehand next time?

I would have requested a different location for these to be served, thus resulting in less commotion regarding such a sensitive subject," Nathan said, his jaw flexing and voice tight.

The man apologized before leaving, and we stood there holding the subpoenas.

I stared down at the envelope, the sound of paper ripping filling my ears.

"What's the party about?" Andrew asked.

Nathan let out a snort. "They want a deposition from us. Seems habitual boy is still spouting it's not his fault, that you provoked him."

Andrew's eyes narrowed on the slip of paper. "Like hell it is."

My chest began tightening, and I concentrated on trying to keep my breathing regulated. It was a good thing; I had to keep repeating that mantra to myself. He was going to be put away for a long time. He would never be able to hurt me again.

My coaching wasn't helping. Doubt started to nag at me, what if's taking over my mind. Adam's voice was in my head, laughing about how nothing could touch him, just as he had said many years before.

"Well, that was a little faster than I anticipated," Nathan said, breaking the silence and opening the envelope, looking over the information. "Looks like it's going to be a speedy trial."

I couldn't speak as dread settled in. Things I hadn't thought about came flooding to me.

I was going to have to retell the whole ordeal to more strangers, under oath. Pandora's Box was going to be opened for all to see; the weak nothingness of a girl who was too stupid to check the peephole.

I began shaking, all of my muscles were clenched tight in fright, and I felt sick.

"Hey, hey," Nathan called, his hands rubbing up and down my arms before he pulled me to him. "Shhh, this is good, remember?"

My knees buckled from under me, and I slumped against him. Pulling me close, he sat on the floor and leaned against the desk as he cradled me in his arms. His hands made soothing circles on my back, while his lips placed tender kisses on my forehead, trailing down my cheek to my lips.

"I'm here, baby. I'll be there with you. I love you, and I won't let him anywhere near you. Him, your father, or Cheryl. Get their voices, their words, out of your head. The only one you need is my voice, telling you how much I love you."

My fingers clenched onto his jacket, my breath coming out in rapid pants. My chest was tight, unable to pull in a full breath.

"She's panicking."

"I know," Nathan said, confirming that I wasn't all right. "Check her purse; she keeps her pills in there."

I was aware of Andrew moving around the desk, but not much else. Nathan was trying to calm me, but his voice was a whisper over the roaring in my ears and everything was starting to fade.

"They're not here!"

"Grab mine, top desk drawer." Nathan directed him.

I tried to center myself, but it snuck up on me. I was choking, trying in desperation to breathe and began to claw at my throat in an attempt to get Adam's hand away that wasn't really there.

"Lila!" Nathan cried out, grabbing my hands.

Then I felt it. The zing, the electricity of Nathan's lips on mine, his fingers digging into my skin as he pulled my body as close to his as he could. A shudder ran through me, and my airway opened back up. My lungs drew in the welcomed air as my heartbeat lessened. Nathan kissed all over my face and neck, grounding me to him, making me *feel* him…and it worked.

My breaths began to regulate, and Nathan pressed a pill into my mouth. He held up a bottle of water and tipped it back.

"Come on, baby, swallow."

It was hard to do as he requested with my chest still stuttering.

As I was pacified, I heard the voices and my head turned to look at the door. About six people, at least two Boob Squad members, stood at the threshold, looking at me, then looking at Nathan, chatting away about us.

"Everybody out! You have no business being here," Andrew yelled, pushing people back and shutting the door.

Jennifer was the last, a murderous gleam in her eye before she stalked off.

The end had come. This was it. No more pretending we hated each other.

I was very clingy that night, unable to leave his touch even for a second, because we both knew what was coming in the morning. One or both of us was going to be jobless by the end of the day.

Nathan kept saying everything was going to be okay, but he wouldn't say more than that. When I brought up talking to Jack, he asked me to let him take care of everything. So, I relented and tried to relax, perched on his lap, straddling his hips.

The next morning we drove together, my fingers tangled in his as we rode the elevator up. We disengaged as the doors opened and we walked into the receptionist area. Libby wasn't in yet, but as we walked past her desk, we found many others were.

We stopped, halted in our tracks by the people staring at us like a sideshow attraction. Whispered words floated around the air, and out of the corner of my eye I saw Nathan's jaw clench.

"Fuck it." He grabbed my hand, dragging me down the hall behind him.

We rushed past the cubes and offices to the other side of the building, to our office. Owen was at his desk just outside as we rounded the corner. He stood and followed behind me as we stepped in.

"How bad is it?" Nathan asked while Owen closed the door behind him.

"It's pretty bad. Jennifer sent out an email, complete with a picture of Lila in your arms and you kissing her."

I stared at Owen, unblinking. "You knew?" I turned to Nathan. "He knew?"

Nathan nodded. "You read us pretty early on, didn't you?"

Owen smirked. "Yeah, I had an inkling in June, but I knew when I started helping out. Nathan wasn't the best at hiding his distress. I was the only one that caught on that your wellbeing was the cause of said distress, and not the extra work. They're so damn vain they can't see past their own reflection."

I wanted to laugh at his observation, but was still too stunned at his admission. "That was almost six months ago! You never told anyone… Why?"

He shrugged his shoulders. "The policy was a bit harsh in my view. Plus, I could see how torn up Nathan was without you. Who am I to stand in the way of true love?"

I walked over to Owen and hugged him, the action surprising all in the room. "Such a sweet guy. Your girlfriend is very lucky to have you."

All morning long, murmured words could be heard as the gossip spread throughout. We tried to block it out, but even our email was loaded with curious people. We didn't leave our office, having Owen fetch anything we needed. The world outside seemed like a foreign place. I had no idea what to do with the attention we were receiving.

We went to lunch together—no point in hiding. Afterward, Nathan left for a meeting with Jack, kissing me before going, leaving me alone with the gawkers and gossips.

At one point I had to venture out as Owen was missing from his desk. The hawks were watching, circling overhead, waiting for someone to emerge.

I was cornered, and they were pissed.

"You always act like you're so high and mighty. Now we see why," Kelly said, a huff in her tone as she spat at me.

Then it was their leader, Jennifer's turn. "Just because Nathan was nice and went out with you a few times and fucked you doesn't mean you're going to go riding off into the sunset together."

My hands balled into fists, and my head pounded as the pressure built up inside while my teeth clenched together. "Really? What about being together for almost ten months and living together for two?"

"L-live together?" Tiffany asked, stuttering in surprise.

I smirked and refused to back down, my spine strengthening at the knowledge they weren't going to beat me down. "Mm-hmm! After my stepbrother attacked me, Nathan insisted I get rid of my place. It was almost like we were living together anyway, so we made it official. I moved in with him. He worries." I shrugged nonchalantly like it was no big deal.

"Beside the point," Jennifer said, changing the subject. "You're gone. They won't keep you over him, so you better start packing, because he is going to leave you in the dust."

"You know, I always wonder…if that is what you really think of him, why are you so desperate to get him? The thrill of the chase? Or is he simply a nice trophy for your bedpost? To me, he's the most wonderful man I've ever met, not just another guy to fuck. Though he is fantastic in that department; I won't lie about that fact."

I didn't even get to enjoy the furious looks on their faces as Nathan came out of nowhere and grabbed my arm, pulling me from them. While he was moving me from their presence, an announcement came over the speakers to meet in the conference room.

People gathered, cramming into what was a small space for the number of people who were coming in.

"Excuse me, can I have everyone's attention? I have a very important announcement to make," Nathan shouted over the crowd to make sure everyone heard him. The room settled down to listen, curiosity winning over. "I know many of you have heard rumors I'm having an affair with my office mate, Delilah Palmer. Well, I'm here to put those rumors to rest. I am not having an affair with her." He then turned to me, smiling at the confused look on my face. "We're in a relationship."

The room burst into whispers and talk, silencing Nathan. My cheeks were red as everyone stared at me. Words of disbelief, "I knew it," and "thought they hated each other," circled around.

"Effective immediately, I have left my position with Holloway and Holloway."

I stared at him in complete shock. He never mentioned anything to me about leaving. My hand tightened on his. I wasn't ready for that. I needed him.

"No! She was the one who was supposed to leave!" Jennifer cried. The other BS members chimed in with agreement.

"Fat chance of that happening, girls." Caroline beamed with pride at them. "Unlike you, Delilah is worth something to the company."

There was a ruckus, and I knew Caroline was about to take a BS down when Jack's voice boomed out for order.

Nathan turned to me and took my other hand, his gaze finding mine.

"I know you won't always be safe with me, but I need you. Over the last ten months, you have come to know me more than anyone. You are my best friend, my lover, my soul mate, the love of my life, savior, my naughty girl, and my sweet Honeybear. I want to show everyone that you're mine and I'm yours," he said, then dropped down to one knee. In one hand he held a small box and opened it up revealing a stunning ring inside. "Delilah Anne Palmer, will you marry me?"

My breath caught in my throat. Gasps filled the room. His words were foreign to my ears. Did he just say what I thought he said, or was I imagining it all? Was he holding a diamond ring in his hand? Oh, dear.

My body started to shake, and Nathan's expression turned to one of panic and fear. He stood and wrapped his arms around me.

"Shh, calm down, baby." His hand made soothing strokes in my hair and down my back.

I clutched onto his suit jacket. "Did you just...*propose*?"

"I did," he replied, pulling back a bit. "I want you to be my wife. I want to make you Lila Thorne. It has such a nice ring to it."

I returned to staring at him before standing on the tips of my toes and wrapping my arms around his neck, kissing him as hard as I could. He pulled me closer, lifting me from the ground.

"Yes!" I cried after releasing him. "Yes, yes, yes. I'll marry you."

He placed a kiss on my neck and drew back to take my lips. The roar of applause filled our ears. After planting my feet back on the ground, he placed the most beautiful diamond solitaire and platinum ring on my left hand.

My right hand covered my mouth as I stared down, holding back sobs of happiness. "It's beautiful."

He beamed down at me. "I'm happy you like it."

We shook a few congratulatory hands before the room returned to a gentle hum.

"If you'll all excuse us, I have a desk to clean out and a fiancée to celebrate with," Nathan said with a smile, wrapping his arm around my waist, pushing his way through the gathered crowd.

"What now?" I questioned as we walked, receiving pats on the back and congratulations as we went.

"Well, I need a new job, and you have a wedding to plan." He could not stop grinning, not that I blamed him. His smile was so large I was afraid it might break his face. I'd never seen him so happy.

I leaned my head against his shoulder as we walked. "So, I guess this means I have a date to the Christmas party?"

"Seeing as we aren't violating office policy any longer, I suppose you do."

Everyone was still milling in the hallways and conference room, gossiping about Nathan's unexpected and shocking proposal. Their heads were still spinning. There would be no one to interrupt us.

He pushed my back against the wall as soon as we made it through the door of our office—his mouth tantalizingly close to my ear. "Now, I think we have some celebrating to do," he whispered as his teeth scraped along my neck. "Where better than the first place I took you?"

His hands were on either side of my thighs, dragging my skirt up and over my ass. I ripped his shirt open, sending buttons pinging around the room.

No more masks to hide behind, no more pretending.

No more breach.

Whatever life hurled our way, we would face it together.

I couldn't wait.

ACKNOWLEDGEMENTS

Special thanks to:

My husband, David, for his support and encouragement in my writing endeavors. Crystal, for without her friendship, support, and guidance I would never have entered this journey. Massy, for being the voice of wisdom and clarity. Stephanie, for sharing is caring. Kyla for her sessions. Nyddi for her unending encouragement and help through this process. Deborah for her support and teachings. Chrisann for her perspective and love of lemons.

Last, but very much not least, to SM for writing a beautiful love story that helped me find the passion in life I was missing, and the fandom for bringing me friends, family and the courage to spread my wings.

Words can never express my gratitude and love to you all.

ABOUT THE AUTHOR

K.I. Lynn is the *USA Today* Bestselling Author from The Bend Anthology and the Amazon Bestsellers, Breach and Becoming Mrs Lockwood. She spent her life in the arts, everything from music to painting and ceramics, then to writing. Characters have always run around in her head, acting out their stories, but it wasn't until later in life she would put them to pen. It would turn out to be the one thing she was really passionate about.

Since she began posting stories online, she's garnered acclaim for her diverse stories and hard hitting writing style. Two stories and characters are never the same, her brain moving through different ideas faster than she can write them down as it also plots its quest for world domination…or cheese. Whichever is easier to obtain… Usually it's cheese.

Website—www.kilynnauthor.com

Facebook—www.facebook.com/kilynn.breach

Twitter—twitter.com/KI_Lynn_

Instagram—www.instagram.com/k.i.lynn

Get my Newsletter—http://bit.ly/1U9NSoC

Becoming Mrs. Lockwood

Every girl has dreams of meeting Prince Charming, or at least I know I did.

A fairy tale-like meeting of love at first site.
Real life and fairy tales are very different.

I'm just a small town Indiana girl that had a chance encounter with one of Hollywood's golden boys. You may think you know where this story goes—not even close.

Life is different. Marriage is hard. It's even worse when you're strangers.

Find out more here:
books2read.com/BecomingMrsLockwood

Six

I had a one-night stand. It wasn't my first, but it would be my last.

A gun to the head.

A trained killer.

A deadly conspiracy.

Kidnapped and on the run, my life and death is in the hands of a sadist captor who happens to be my one-night stand. Armed with countless weapons, money, and new identities, the man I call Six drags me around the world.

The manhunt is on and Six is the next target. Can we find out who is killing off the Cleaners before they find us?

Two down, seven to go.

When it's all over he'll finish the job that dropped him into my life, and end it.

Stockholm Syndrome meets bucket list, and the question of what would you do to live before you died. The questions aren't always answered in black and white. Gray becomes the norm as my morals are tested.

Death is a tragedy, and I'll do anything to stay alive.

Are you ready for the last ride of your life? Six has a gun to your head—what would you do?

This isn't a love story.

It's a death story.

Find out more here: books2read.com/Six-KILynn
Check out the Trailer: youtu.be/fzpON3PadIA

The Executive

Business is king, and I have an empire to topple.

Ivy is my new assistant and a threat to me. She's my undoing. If ever I was to believe in a cosmic connection, it was the moment I met her.

For years I've had one goal--revenge. As CEO, I have crafted a strategic plan for business, but never a life beyond.

With one touch from her, the veil is lifted. Things are different, and every moment I'm near her, my world begins to change.

A wall of propriety keeps me from her. I need her as my pawn in this war, beside me in battle. Sharing the secrets of my enemies, and her desires in my bed. Her body to claim as mine.

Getting what I want has consequences.

Collateral damage is real.

In the game of crushing kings of men, I never planned on my heart being a sacrifice.

Find out more here:
books2read.com/TheExecutive

Cocksure

A life altering lie, ten years, and one wild night later, the game has changed.

Niko

My life is great. I love my job, have awesome friends, and a great family.

Women love me, even if they know it's just for a night.

I always thought love at first sight was bullshit. Then she came storming into my life. She tore through my every rule, rocked my world, and knocked me on my ass.

There's only one problem…she lied.+

Turns out my best friend's little sister isn't so little anymore.

Everly

I stole a night with my fantasy. Lied to him.

After ten years of not seeing each other, Niko doesn't even recognize me.

So I take what I want from him, what I need from him. Without worry. Without consequence.

What I didn't count on was the lingering need for him.

Once the truth is out, the game changes. There are consequences.

I should have known nothing in my life is ever simple.

My brother is going to kill his best friend and I have nine months to figure out what I want.

Find out more here: books2read.com/Cocksure-Lynn-Kelley

Need, Book 1

I was Kira's from the first moment I saw her. Maybe it was love at first sight, but I was only ten.

She became my best friend.

My crush.

The girl I can't live without.

But I have to.

She was almost mine, but my father took away my chance.

Now she lives across the hall from me. Instead of the title of girlfriend, she's now my stepsister.

But that doesn't stop how I feel, how I want her. Thankfully, I'm off to college two hundred miles away, but even that doesn't help.

She's under my skin, all around me, and I watch her morph from a sexy teenager to an irresistible woman.

I can't take it anymore, I need her.

Is it possible to ever be happy without the one person you *need*?

"I'm Brayden, baby. The man you've been dreaming about your whole life. And I'm about to fucking show you why."

Part 1 of a 3 part series.

Find out more here: books2read.com/NeedSeries

www.ingramcontent.com/pod-product-compliance
Lightning Source LLC
Chambersburg PA
CBHW032124180726

48284CB00002B/683